# DO ALIENS READ SCI-FI?

# RUTH MASTERS

**Do Aliens Read Sci-Fi?**
**by Ruth Masters**

First published 2011, re-published June 2023

© Ruth Masters

ISBN: 979-8387018305

Originally published under the author's previous name, Ruth Wheeler

The right of Ruth Masters to be identified as the author of this work has been asserted by her in accordance with the Copyright, Designs and Patents Act 1988.

All rights reserved. No part of this publication may be reproduced, stored in or introduced into a retrieval system, or transmitted, in any form, or by any means (electronic, mechanical, photocopying, recording or otherwise) without the prior written permission of the publisher. Any person who does any unauthorised act in relation to this publication may be liable to criminal prosecution and civil claims for damages.

Cover by Tim Hirst

This book is sold subject to the condition that it shall not, by way of trade or otherwise, be lent, re-sold, hired out, or otherwise circulated without the publisher's prior consent in any form of binding or cover other than that in which it is published and without a similar condition including this condition being imposed on the subsequent purchaser.

# CHAPTER 1

Tom Bowler examined the small capsule cupped in his left hand. The abstemious pill. He had experienced so much in the few weeks he had been living on the planetoid Truxxe. He had learned a lot in such a short time and met so many new and interesting people. He wondered how the people back on Earth would marvel at such precious inventions as this small capsule.

His thoughts this morning, however, were a little cloudy. His head was spinning and his gait, unsteady. Yet his condition was eased at the promise of welcome sobriety after the self-administration of the abstemious pill. He wet his lips and dropped the capsule into his mouth. Before he could relax into wellness, Tom knew that first he would have to endure two long minutes of discomfort and nausea while the pill took effect. Eyes screwed shut, face contorted in pain, stomach swimming with sickness; Tom let the waves of his condensed hangover wash over his mind and body in an unbearable queasy ocean. Head hammering, guts lurching, he felt his knees give as he crumpled to the floor.

He lay there for a moment, foetal-like.

Soon, the flow of nausea ebbed away and a great calmness and sense of normality crept upon him. His brain had stopped pounding against the inside of his skull, his vision was clear, and his mind was focussed.

Blinking, he stood erect and smiled at the Truxxian Raphyl, his colleague and friend.

"Feeling better, Tombo?" Raphyl asked him.

"Yeah, much better. It must have been a good night last night.' Tom grinned.

"Not bad," Raphyl concurred and returned the abstemious pill packet to the medicine cabinet.

"I suppose we'd better go and serve some burgers before the supervisor arrives." Tom trudged towards the staff room door which led out to the restaurant.

Tom Bowler had arrived on the wandering planetoid Truxxe after inadvertently applying for a job at a fast food counter in a service station somewhere between the Andromeda and Triangulum galaxies. He had wanted to take a year out in the real world before following his parents' wishes and applying to university. He wasn't really sure whether this would be considered the *real* world exactly – for it was another world entirely. A world like no other that he had ever imagined existed when he was living in a small Worcestershire town in England. Tom was continually amazed at the number and variety of beings which passed through the service station on this richly resourced world. So many creatures from so many worlds, stopping off to rest in one of Truxxe's Superior Services hotel suites, refuel their spaceship or simply order a burger from the Express Cuisine where Tom worked. There was so much out here that Earth didn't know about and yet Truxxe constantly reminded Tom of Earth. There were cafes, fuel stations, clothes shops and swimming pools. There were clubs bars, restaurants, music shops and shops and sports.

Tom had never been the sporty type, having historically being entertained by computer games, concerts and science fiction and fantasy novels. But here he was something of a sporting hero. He had recognition in the game of Spotoon. The set-up was comparable to that of a darts match, with participants taking turns at effectively spitting from a chalked line, or oche, at a disc bearing a target of three coloured rings. Tom was still amazed that there was actually a distinguished sport involving sputum — long-distance spitting was a skill which he and his friend Nathan had reserved for their childish games of mild vandalism; scoring points for hitting various vehicles from bridges over roads and rivers. Here, it seemed, it was acceptable and indeed *creditable* to celebrate such skills. Here, humans could reach distances that most otherworldly inhabitants struggled to reach, apart from the best spotoon players. Another way in which Spotoon reminded Tom of darts, was its association with intoxicating beverages as it was essentially a pub game.

Which brings us to why Tom felt the worse for wear. He had played a match with his team, Hasprin's Legion, the previous evening. It had been a friendly against fellow team the Gharka in bar Six Seven, the popular recreational meeting place Tom and his friends frequented. The bar was open between the sixth and seventh hour of the ten-hour day (or rotation), as the name suggested. The team's leader, Ghy Hasprin, had most generously bought several celebratory rounds of drinks, for both teams, after their victory. Raphyl, although a non-player, had joined the team after their game and so the two of them were glad to access the staff room medicine cabinet that morning.

"Morning Tom," Kayleesh, the beautiful Augtopian greeted him as he reached the counter. He smiled at her sheepishly.

"Hello Kayleesh." He punched in the access code, which initiated the till. Kayleesh was looking as perky and jovial as ever, Tom noticed. Her golden tresses were shimmering under the bright lights of the restaurant. She eagerly took an order from her first customer - a Truxxian with a food request almost as long as his purple beard. In contrast, Raphyl was slumped over his till, evidently struggling to stay awake despite taking an abstemious pill taken only moments earlier. Tom wondered how Raphyl would cope on Earth with a real hangover. He would not have been able to cope with working with greasy food, he was sure of that. An approaching customer glanced momentarily at the jaded Raphyl before opting for Tom's till.

"Two burgers, a carbonated fruit drink and a ruffleberry milkshake please."

The morning went well, the restaurant being not too quiet, and not too hectic, just the way Tom liked it. After lunchtime, the flow of patrons slowed. Raphyl took the opportunity to excuse himself and sauntered off in the direction of the staff sanitation room. Kayleesh approached Tom, as though she had been waiting for a suitable moment. She had a curious look in her violet eyes, as though she wasn't quite sure how he was going to react to what he had to say.

"Er… Tom, do you… do you remember what you told me in bar Six Seven that time? You know, it was when we were celebrating Hasprin's Legion doing well in the match." What had he said? He couldn't remember. That was weeks ago. He could barely remember the evening before. Had he embarrassed himself? Noticing his perplexity, Kayleesh elaborated.

"You had been talking to Raphyl. He had been drinking rather a lot and had… disclosed to you that he might have come from the past. Do you remember telling me?" Half relieved, Tom smiled. He had forgotten telling her, although he had remembered Raphyl's disclosure. He had, however, since dismissed the conversation, believing it to be merely pub-talk.

"I remember, yeah," he said, awkwardly, fiddling with a spot on his chin. "He was probably just messing around. You know Raphyl." He shrugged.

"Hmm I'm not so sure," Kayleesh deliberated. "I've been thinking about it ever since. I wonder if he was telling the truth." Tom gave her a doubtful look before he was drawn from the conversation by a family of fervent green-haired creatures advancing towards the counter.

Hannond Putt was on holiday and he was smiling. He hadn't had a holiday in a long time. Enjoying the warming rays of the Radiakkan suns on his bare, hairy chest; dipping his toes in the cool cyan-blue ocean and listening to the Wakkinali birds cawing overhead, he was very happy indeed. And what was more, his older brother Schlomm Putt wasn't with him. No being bullied, no plotting, no scheming. Just himself and a bottle of Glorbian whiskey for ten whole rotations.

Hannond's broad grin widened under his hairy lip at the thought. His stubby toes wiggled in the refreshing water as he took a sip of his cool drink. He sighed. This was what life was supposed to be like, he mused, as though he were the first holiday maker to ever have had that thought. He thought about when their father had bequeathed the brothers his meat-distribution company, a lucrative business. But rather than simply enjoying the inherited company and reaping the benefits, as Hannond wanted, all Schlomm endeavoured to do was plot away at unscrupulous methods of acquiring yet more money. Somehow Hannond always seemed to get involved, reluctant though he was. His older brother was so influential and domineering that he often convinced him that his ideas were good ones, even though Hannond knew it was always he who ended up getting his hands dirty (and Glorbian hands were already grubby enough).

Happily, Schlomm had agreed, after their previous unsuccessful venture, that the two of them should have a holiday; apart. So, while his sibling was strutting round some murky swamp somewhere, or whatever he was doing — Hannond had decided not to care —Hannond was here on a stunning beach in one of the smallest continents on the beautiful planet Radiakka. Hannond Putt was wearing his favourite sash, stretched across his stout, globular body. Coarse, auburn hair carpeted the entirety of his skin, which was turning a light tan in the heat of the suns. He realised how much so when a fellow tourist apparently mistook him for a larger than average coconut. Disappointed that it wasn't a refreshing nut resting on the shore being lapped by the waves, the tourist had sloped off hungry, and a little embarrassed.

# CHAPTER 2

Tom was getting ready to leave his post at the end of his shift when suddenly a long, orange hand appeared on his shoulder. Startled, he spun round to face its owner. Mayty Reeston, the Express Cuisine's chef and Tom's teammate, was grinning at him.

"Before you go," he said, deliberately glancing at his timepiece. "I just wanted to let you know that there's a match coming up in a few rotations." Tom nodded his understanding.

"Who is it against?"

"It's a friendly against BBs," he said matter-of-factly.
Tom gulped. That phrase was oxymoronic at best. BBs didn't do friendly. He raised an eyebrow.

Mayty laughed. "It's nothing to worry about, Tom, they've been knocked down a hook or two since being disqualified from the last Big Match anyway. If anything, they'll be grovelling." Tom was unconvinced, however.

"Well, I just hope it's somewhere public and not in Ghy's apartment or anywhere that a fight might break out. Again."

"I don't think BBs care whether they start a fight in public." Mayty's round, orange face grinned.

"You're hardly helping your case, here." Tom shook his head, laughing. "OK, well… thanks for the warning." Mayty tilted his head at Tom. Tom returned the gesture with a forced smile and continued on to his quarters.

He was looking forward to getting out of his uniform and into his recreational compsuit. Far from being restrictive, Truxxe's Superior Services regulation uniform consisted of a long, flowing blue robe, which Tom wore over shorts as he hated the thought of having bare legs. By contrast, putting on a compsuit was comparable to stepping into a wetsuit. The Wardrobian Effect that worked within the complex caused all wearers of compsuits to seemingly blend in with their environment and be accepted by - and accepting of - the attire of other wearers. The idea was to make the employees and visitors feel comfortable in this cosmopolitan setting. For example, the Effect caused Tom to view all manner of aliens as though they were dressed in denim jeans and dark hooded sweaters emblazoned with band names; outfits he was familiar with amongst people from his own subculture on his home world. However, Tom found the whole experience hilarious rather than comforting. The image of huge be-tentacled beings from the ocean planet of Fraffinasia wearing a Stone Roses hoody and multi-legged faded jeans was a difficult one to elude. Keeping a straight face was not always easy. Even if Fraffinasians laughed with their tonsils lolling by their aquatic limbs, the correct meaning of Tom's expressions were translated by the building's ALSID (Atmospheric Linguistic Spectrum Interpretation Device) unit so they would know if he were trying to stifle a smirk. The main reason Tom wore his suit was so that he didn't appear too strange to others. He often wondered how they saw him. He hated to admit it, but he was conforming.

Once he had got changed, Tom made his way to his bathroom and used the ergonomic toilet, which formed itself in a disturbingly biddable way around his rear, to accommodate his "alien" body. He still hadn't quite got used to the way the furniture insisted on doing this — the toilet in particular still sent a shiver down his spine. He washed his hands and swilled his face in cool, refreshing water. He went back into the main room of his quarters and slumped onto his bed. He wondered what he should do that evening. His team had no plans for a spot of Spotoon that evening and he had already eaten at work. He gazed at the blank, pale blue wall ahead of him, which was exceedingly deficient in anything resembling a television. He longed to watch one of his favourite sci-fi series, music videos or comedy dramas. Even a news bulletin would do. He thought about Ghy Hasprin's quarters which had been generously kitted out with a bar, Spotoon board and some kind of stereo system. He missed music. Tom hadn't heard much of what passed for music here on Truxxe, except for the bagpipe-folk-rock hybrid channelled through the speakers at bar Six Seven. He found its rhythm to be too extraordinary to be enjoyable, exactly. Perhaps he'd ask Raphyl where he could buy a stereo system and find out whether there was more than one music genre available on this planetoid. A sharp knock at the door broke his thoughts.

"Tom?" It was Kayleesh. He jumped up suddenly. His uniform was slovenly left on the table. His underwear was draped over a chair. Worst still, an unsavoury waft was emanating from the bathroom.

"Wait a minute… er… a krom," he corrected himself. Quickly, he scooped up an armful of clothes and shut them in a cupboard on the far side of the room. He waved his hand rapidly and fruitlessly, willing the unwelcome bathroom smells to dissipate. Taking a deep breath, he let his female friend into his apartment. "Sorry about that," he said, noticing Kayleesh reflexively wrinkle her nose as she entered. Oh well, there was little he could do about it now. What did she expect, turning up at a bachelor pad unannounced - mountain-fresh air freshener and paper doilies?

"Want one?" she proffered a packet of some kind of snack biscuits. Tom shook his head and she casually helped herself to a seat, the blue ergonomic seat adjusting beneath her as she did so. "Sorry to just turn up at your door Tom,' she smiled at him sweetly and bit into one of the biscuits. It was green. Whatever flavour was it? Tom almost wished he had accepted. He shrugged off her statement.

"That's OK I wasn't doing anything," his face flushed bright red.    "Er… I mean I had nothing planned." He saw her notice him blushing again. This frequent colour-change whenever he spoke to her seemed to amuse the pale-faced Kayleesh for some reason. She didn't comment, however.

"I just wanted to talk to you about what I was saying today — about Raphyl," she said.

"Shouldn't you be talking to Raphyl about this?"

"Well not really, because I'm not supposed to know about it, am I? It was you he told. He's never mentioned it before so it's obviously not the kind of thing he goes around telling people is it? He'd had a lot of Truxxian gloop that night before his lips were loosened. Even for Raphyl."

"Then why do you want to know more? I don't think he'd be willing to talk about it, do you? You know Raphyl. He'd just get all stroppy like last time."

"I want to know why he's so secretive about his past. Aren't you interested, Tom?"

"Everything's a quest to you isn't it, Kayleesh? You may have helped unravel the mysteries of the origins of Truxxe but getting into Raphyl's head is a different assignment altogether!"

"Well, you know me — I like a challenge." The beautiful Augtopian grinned and took a bite of her biscuit. She looked irresistible. He succumbed.

"OK, OK. I'll ask him. But don't be disappointed if he doesn't want to talk." Kayleesh beamed. "Thanks Tom. Find out what you can then we'll go on from there." She stood up to leave.

Go on to where? What was she planning to do? Dig up his family tree? Send him back to his own time? He sighed, bewildered, and saw her to the door. She hurried off along the corridor, a trail of green biscuit crumbs in her wake.

Schlomm Putt was on holiday and he was grumpy. He wanted to relax but his conscience wouldn't let him. The demand for meat was steady, his business was surviving, more than surviving in fact, but that wasn't enough for Schlomm. He wanted riches, he wanted excitement, he wanted greater riches. He'd given up on the idea of Glorbian gem smuggling since his previous escapade. He'd certainly given up on trusting Strellions and had almost given up on relying on his brother. Perhaps he'd manage better without Hannond this time. Although somehow Hannond always managed to muscle his way into his plans — and always managed to get half of the profits. Well this time that wouldn't happen. He'd cope without the encumbrance of his brother, who was safely several light-years away on the planet Radiakka, no doubt lazing about in the sun supping Glorbian whiskey.

The following evening, Tom Bowler and Raphyl were spending their spare time and spare Ds at bar Six Seven. Modestly decorated, the soft yellow lighting complemented the relaxed atmosphere of the social venue. The music was loud, but not so loud that they had to shout in order to be heard. The bar ran along part of the far wall, behind which Lan, a native Truxxian, served various intoxicating substances according to the species of customer. The Spotoon board, currently unoccupied, spied from the wall of a sparsely seated section of the room like an immense eye. Tom was on his second lager and Raphyl had already downed four tripedal glasses of Truxxian gloop, which he held between his elongated digits.

Tom didn't want to overdo his alcohol intake this evening. If he was going to interrogate Raphyl to satisfy Kayleesh's curiosity, he would need to remember what he learned and therefore wanted to remain moderately clear-headed. He was doubly glad that Raphyl appeared to want to achieve the opposite effect; perhaps he'd be a more willing orator. Tom and Raphyl partook in their usual inane banter before Tom broached the more serious subject, in as matter-of-fact tone as he could muster.

"Hey, Raph, where was it you said you were from again? I remember you mentioning something about where... or when..." he paused and waited for a reaction. Raphyl raised his purple monobrow and his dark eyes searched Tom's face.

"I did?" he sounded surprised. He looked down at his drink. "Uh... maybe I did, yeah. Ah... you don't want to know about that, Tombo." Raphyl took a gulp from his glass, all too casually. Tom thought he was going to say something else, but he remained silent. The lilac fox-glove-skinned being had an intense expression on his face. His gaze was focussed at a point behind Tom, although his thoughts were obviously elsewhere Wasn't it normally girls who were bothered about all this soul-searching nonsense? Why was he doing this? Tom furrowed his brow and took a long pull of his drink. Why didn't Miss Curious ask him herself if she was so interested? Girls really were alien to him — this one, literally. He opened his mouth, about to apologise and make a joke about it, but to his surprise, Raphyl responded.

"OK Tombo. You've told me about your home planet and how you got here by some bizarre misunderstanding. It's only fair I tell you how *I* got here I suppose. But once I do, you're in on it too," he said ominously. He stood up without warning. Tom realised he was going to the bar to refuel his glass.

Tom waited, impatiently. Raphyl, as usual, made no attempts at rushing this errand and returned a full fifteen kroms later. Tom was about to moan at him when he realised that he was carrying two glasses, one brimming with lager. He hadn't planned to have another, but Tom didn't complain at his friend's generosity. "Sorry, I saw Jephle at the bar. You know what he's like when he gets talking," he said by way of an apology. No, he didn't know — the chef had barely said two words to Tom during his residence on Truxxe, but he let it pass. Raphyl took a long, purposeful mouthful of Truxxian gloop before he spoke again.

"You know how you don't want your parents to know the truth about where you're actually living and working?" Tom nodded. His parents were still under the illusion that he was working at a burger bar in a motorway service station in Exeter. They would never believe the truth. "Well, I don't want anyone to know I'm here either," he looked around suspiciously, as though he hadn't frequented this establishment most evenings for who knew how long. He leaned across the table and said in hushed tones, "I'm hiding."

"Hiding? At TSS?" Tom absent-mindedly began his third pint, utterly flummoxed. Raphyl shook his head.

"I'm hiding in the future! Well… my future."

"How? Why?"

Raphyl leaned closer still until their glasses clinked together, clumsily. He whispered the simple phrase,

"I'm wanted."

# CHAPTER 3

The flavoursome, succulent aroma of baked volubabeast filled the air. A stream of saliva seeped out of the corner of Hannond's expectant mouth. He licked his thick lips and wondered if there was any sauce to accompany his meal. He wondered who was cooking it and how big a slice he could expect to receive.

Suddenly, pain.

Hannond awoke and noticed that his skin was burning. It wasn't volubabeast which was cooking, it was him! His skin wasn't merely hot - a fully-fledged forest fire was progressing across his hairy body. Horrified, he instinctively rolled towards the direction of the sea, expecting the cool waters to extinguish the burning flesh on his little rotund body. But the intensity of the suns was dazzling him and so he didn't see that the tide had gone out. Like some kind of deranged, screaming Catherine wheel ablaze, he rolled across the hot sands. Where was the sea? He glimpsed a vacated beach towel as he tumbled. Would it help pat out the flames as he passed over it? No, it only served to catch fire as Hannond tumbled across the arid material, hopelessly. Finally, the beach incline plateaued, and he came to a stop. He was still, however, on fire. Thoroughly naked now, what was left of his sash having fused to his fur he stood and looked around him, panicking. He was still some distance from the mocking surf of the ocean's edge. Until - saved! There was a blanket right where he had come to a halt. Quickly, he wrapped the thing around him and dropped to the floor (not that the short creature had far to drop). He rolled around once more until he was certain the flames had ceased. As he came to rest, a grinning, humanoid child emptied a yellow plastic bucket of seawater splashing needlessly over his head. The toddler laughed gleefully and ran off in the opposite direction, bucket swinging in hand.

Singed and sodden, but enormously relieved, Hannond got back to his feet. His respite was short-lived, however.

"Sacrilegious beast!" a voice boomed. "Heretical monster! Profane fiend!" When Hannond had had quite enough of the synonyms, he looked about him, thoroughly disgruntled, trying to detect who was venting these harsh opinions in his direction. Suddenly a large, indigo hand snatched the scorched blanket from around Hannond's torso. It was then that the naked Glorbian noticed that it was not a blanket at all. His mouth fell open. He realised the reason for the insults of the owner of the indigo hand; a native of Radiakka.

"How dare you desecrate the Radiakkan transnational flag!" spat the absurdly vexed Radiakkan. Pronounced eyes ran their glare up and down the length of the blackened cloth in angered disbelief. He shook the flag with vigour, in an attempt to emphasise this act of vandalism. Hannond simply opened and shut his mouth a few times, unsure of what to say. Radiakkans were ludicrously patriotic. He could no more protest his innocence had he been caught with a knife embedded in the chest of a native. The fact that he hadn't realised what he was using to plainly save his own life would not be a viable excuse—not in the view of a Radiakkan anyway.

"Have you nothing to say, Glorbian?" The violet-blue individual glared at him, his goggle eyes burning a hole in him more intense than the combined heat of the two suns.

"I didn't know — I never would have knowingly…"

"Ignorance is no excuse," he boomed, giving the flag another shake for good measure. Soon the indigo creature was joined by two more indigo creatures — wearing Radiakkan police uniforms.

"We'll take it from here," one of them said, his voice surprisingly high-pitched. He looked at the singed blanket with as much disgust and horror as the first man. He looked down at Hannond with even more revulsion, if that was possible. "Sir, you're under arrest."

Tom looked at his friend. "Wanted?" he repeated. "Why? Who by? What have you done?"

"I'm a fugitive." Raphyl leant back a little. Tom's eyebrows disappeared into his hairline. Raphyl's voice was still low. "It's all a big misunderstanding really. I doubt they're still looking for me… well actually they can't still be looking for me because they'd be dead by now. About three hundred years dead, in fact." He took a gulp of his drink

"So, what did you do? Or what do they think you did?" Raphyl took in a long breath.

"Hey, Tom!" came the familiar tones of Ghy Hasprin. Tom looked up from the discussion and sighed, inwardly. With gritted teeth he responded, as amicably as possible.

"Ghy." He really wished his team captain hadn't picked that moment to appear. Raphyl's imminent disclosure was within his grasp. They exchanged the team greeting which involved the tilting of the head to one side, pointing the ear in the direction of the other person – which was easier for some species than others.

"Just the two of you out tonight?" Ghy's great crimson bulk overshadowed the small, round table. His great, ruby-skinned head was supported by a thick, veiny neck. The Spotoon player transported his amply built, tapered torso over to a nearby chair. Having no legs, Ghy's weight was carried solely by two, huge, burly arms. He hauled his chair across so that he could join the two Express Cuisine workers at their small table.

"Yeah," Tom replied. "Just a couple of drinks after work, you know." Tom looked at Raphyl, agitatedly, who didn't seem particularly put out by this interruption. Tom found his friend's serenity and lack of urgency infuriating. Couldn't he just spit it out now? What had Raphyl done that was so bad that he was a fugitive? He could tell Ghy to go away, that this discussion was private, but he didn't want to arouse suspicion — any hint that Raphyl had a secret and he might be reluctant to divulge anything to Tom after all. So Tom waited. He had no choice. He politely refused drink offers from the team captain, choosing to make the one Raphyl had bought him last. He bided his time. He just couldn't get the burning questions out of his mind. He felt as though he were going to explode if he didn't satisfy the answers he now craved.

Oh Kayleesh. It was all her nosy fault.

Time passed and before Tom realised it, deep in conversation with Ghy about Spotoon matters, Raphyl had sloped off back to his apartment. The chance had been lost.

The following rotation was Truxxe's equivalent of a weekend day. For every seven rotations at work, there were three free rotations which Tom always looked forward to as much as any employee. He hadn't quite acclimatised entirely to the planetoid's ten-hour days, feeling sure that he was missing on some sleep somewhere or other. The hours were longer than on Earth and the decimalisation was certainly easy for him to work out. He knew that physical suitability of foreign employees was considered with regards to the gravity, breathable gasses and environment which they were used to. Therefore, he figured that body-clock too would also be taken into some consideration when selecting candidates. He was certainly glad that he didn't work on a planet whose days were perhaps comparable to fifty Earth hours.

The weekend also meant it was pay day and so Tom decided to go shopping for a music system. The service station which comprised TSS was abundant with all manner of stores, outlets and services. Raphyl had suggested Tom buy a basic melody mech, which would be suitable for his apartment and would hold enough memory for ten thousand songs. He doubted that there were ten songs on Truxxe which he would actually like, let alone ten thousand. Raphyl had even told him of a simple method he used for copying tunes onto blank cards. That way Tom would be able to get a good start on his alien music collection after the sole initial outlay for the device. With some form of entertainment in his possession, Tom would at least be able to invite people to his living quarters with more than a blank wall for entertainment.

Amid the crowds of shoppers — employees and visitors alike — Tom made his way around the rat run of shop-lined walkways. Brightly lit with holographic signs and audible advertisements, the stores all vied for his attention.

"Shoe Fit In – Fit in with our generic compshoes. Why buy the whole suit?" one neon-bright caption read, invading half of the corridor, the lettering dancing majestically and almost illegibly above his head.

"Ten hour all-you-can-eat Drontobuffet – food like father used to make," another shouted from a restaurant window, loud in both volume and colour.   Then Tom found it.

"Harmonious Sounds - melody mechs for beings with ears." The store was abundant with electronic devices ranging in size from the smallness of a pea to the Goliath-like proportions of Ghy Hasprin. He inspected one of the portable, personal devices with curiosity. It was compact and smart looking with something resembling headphones attached, with no less than eight oddly shaped earpieces.

"Ah, I don't think the MD500 would be suitable for your... humanoid ears... unless you are browsing for a gift?" a salesman addressed him, parenthetically. He looked at the salesman who was dressed in the same blue, flowing trademark TSS uniform Tom himself wore for serving burgers and milkshakes. Tom also noticed that the employee had four trumpet-like protrusions on either side of his grey moon-shaped head. When Tom spoke, he waggled them in his direction, their tiny apertures gaping and closing.

"I was just looking," he said. Damned salesmen! You can't escape their interfering in your business, even on an extra solar planet! Then, realising he'd be in this alien shop for the rest of the day if he didn't have some clue as to what he was looking for, he decided to make use of the intrusive member of staff. "I'm looking for a melody mech for my apartment. Could you point me in the right direction?"

"Singular or plural?"

"Er..."

"Would you be wishing to listen alone or accompanied?" he said, hiding his impatience at the ignorance of this foreigner through a forced smile.

"Accompanied I suppose — what's the difference?"

"About twenty Ds. Now, if you will follow me…" Moonface whirled around, his gown whipping Tom's legs as he did so. Tom shrugged and followed, obediently.

The melody mech suited his room. The pale blue walls complemented the smart, silver casing of the device which was prominently displayed on the once-bare wall of his bachelor pad. Now it looked like he was here to stay. This was his home. He had entertainment. But most of all he had something of his own in this apartment, something to show for all those weeks spent behind that serving counter. OK so he didn't have any actual music to play on the thing as yet, but it looked good and that was certainly a start. He fiddled with the various switches and buttons on the mech's fascia, observing the results on the holographic display set up on a separate horizontal panel on his dining table. Tom of course disregarded the manual as would many a young, male human.

Tom recognised the urgency of an excited knock at his door. What now? Always interruptions! He sighed and opened the door. Kayleesh was standing there in her compsuit, an expression of alarm on her face.

"Tom! Raphyl's been arrested!"

# CHAPTER 4

Schlomm's Glorbian timepiece was flashing, clunking and buzzing in the chaotic manner of a Glorbian timepiece, lacking the sophistication of the Truxxian brand. Who was bothering him on his holiday?

Hannond? What does he want?

"What is it? Can't manage without me already? It's been what, seven hours?" he grumbled gruffly.

There was a pause, as though his brother was trying to find the right words.

"I've had a change of h-holiday destination," Hannond's voice stammered.

"OK, fine so I won't be picking you up from Radiakka in a few rotations then — where are you now?" he asked rather crossly and then quipped, "Radiakka not hot enough for you?"

"Oh, it was hot enough all right. I don't think you'll need to collect me for… ooh… the equivalent of another seventy-five Glorbian rotations," Hannond replied.

"Seventy-five rotations? That's a rather long extended holiday, Hannond. And just where are you planning to spend all that time?" the scruffier sibling trumpeted. There was a pregnant pause, which seemed like a lifetime for the impatient Schlomm.

"The planet Porriduum," came the low reply. "And it's not exactly a holiday as much as a jail sentence."

Planet Porriduum was a prison planet. It orbited the pulsar neutron star Gorgon. Gorgon consisted almost entirely of neutrons and had a mass twice that of Earth's sun Sol, although its radius was a mere 10 kilometres.

Residing in the outer edges of the Triangulum galaxy, for centuries Porriduum had served as an intergalactic planet for the incarceration of murderers, bandits and spaceship hijackers of the surrounding galaxies. There was no escape from Porriduum. Residents were doomed to eat watery oatmeal until the end of their sentence on this reviled planet. Doomed to eat porridge. Porridge doomed.

This undesirable world was a hundred per cent inaccessible ninety-nine per cent of the time and only one per cent accessible one per cent of the time. That was unless you wanted to risk being blasted by radiation from the highly focussed beam of its pulsar star. And as Gorgon's beam traversed across the entire planet every two seconds, there wasn't a sufficient window even for the fastest of crafts. The only way to and from this ensnared place was during a total solar eclipse and even then, this narrow gap was heavily guarded, and this sporadic thoroughfare was infested with the to-ing and fro-ing of prison-ships. The small region of terrain which was protected from the lethal beam during an eclipse, this Gorgon's eye, had to be entered using a direct course by the prison-ships during this infinitesimal timeslot. Worse still, the entire surface of the planet, subjected to such immense heat, was forever changing. Melting and reforming, constantly bombarded with the relentless sun's radioactive discharges, the intermittently viscous state of the crust was the only way through to the underground entrance of the gigantic prison buried deep within Porriduum's shell. Once a ship had passed through the molten layers to the access area, it would be trapped in the prison until the radiation melted the surface once more, cyclically encased in the very crust of the planet. The navigators, pilots and astronomers involved in the planning of these assignments were exceptional as were all crew involved—even the flight attendants on these missions were beyond compare. It is unsurprising, then, that exactly zero escapees had ever gotten further than the low orbit of Porriduum without being caught, fried, suffocated or disintegrated. It is also unsurprising that Hannond was not looking forward to being a resident on this famously uninviting planet.

"What? How do you know? How did they catch him?" Tom's mind was racing. Was this linked with what his friend had started to confess to him the previous evening? He never did get to find out any details. What poor timing. He gulped. What if Raphyl's arrest had been *because* of the almost confession? Was it in fact Tom's fault for pushing him into his explanation? His heart sank. Sorry Raph. He looked at Kayleesh, her expression of worry and guilt mirrored his own. He sank back into the chair which morphed submissively, cradling him.

"I don't know how they caught him, but Tyrander is storming about the restaurant with a face like a Radiakkan storm." Tyrander.
Tom pictured his boss, his already bloated, purple flushed face with its trademark expression of thunder — even when he was in one of his jovial moods. He imagined the disconcerting roar of a voice positively sonic booming with fury at finding out that one of his employees was a criminal. Tom gulped again.

"I was going to put in a few extra hours at work today," Kayleesh continued, "but when I saw that Tyrander was out of his office I knew that something had happened. Lucsha Haphreys, the weekend chef, explained to me that police had been on the premises only moments earlier."

"Police? I don't think I've ever seen police at TSS," Tom realised, frowning.

"No, you probably wouldn't notice if you had, Tom. They wear compsuits when they're patrolling the service station. TSS has a relatively low crime rate, so when something like this happens, it's big news," she said, seriously.

"So, what happens now? Is there some kind of holding cell on the station while he awaits trial?" Perhaps they could go and visit him.

"Oh Tom, he'll most likely be on his way to Porriduum at the next available window!"

Far from his dreams of baked volubabeast, the aroma of the unrecognisable contents of the plastic tray reminded him of his older brother's laundry pile. Not that Schlomm had ever actually done any laundry. Although Glorbians were notoriously unhygienic and unkempt, Hannond felt uncomfortably tainted in this filthy, neglected carrying pod.

He hoped that the cells would be more habitable. He prodded the uninspiring looking balls of grey mush which passed for his main meal of the day. He always thought it would be Schlomm who would end up on Porriduum. It would be much more fitting. Schlomm was the real criminal — the one with all the ideas, the instigator. Hannond just fell into situations. And here he was, not even involved in one of his brother's scams and he was on a prison ship destined for Gorgon's solar system.

He didn't know how far it was from Radiakka to Porriduum. He wasn't aware of what kind of propulsion system this craft used and therefore how long it would take to travel to Triangulum. He didn't even know when the next window was to grant access to the prison planet. When was the next solar eclipse? So many unknowns. Perhaps Schlomm would find a way to rescue him. If he wanted adventure, this would be his perfect opportunity: Operation *Saving brother Hannond*. He looked at his chubby wrist with a sigh. His timepiece had been commandeered and replaced with a red prisoner tag. Well, he had wanted some time alone. He couldn't be much more alone that he was at that moment.

Tom's jaw dropped further and further, his eyes still wider, as Kayleesh detailed the reality of where their friend was heading. The reality hit him that Raphyl was most likely on his way to a planet trapped by its own star. What an appalling place it sounded. How was he going to get away from there? Would Tom ever see the idle Truxxian again?

"So how long do people get sent there for, usually?"

"It depends on the crime and also on the rules governed by the planet on which the crime was committed," she shrugged. "Unfortunately, we don't know what crime Raphyl is supposed to be accountable for."

"So, we might never hear from him again?" Tom raised his eyebrows.

"Well… he'll be allowed one call… to his next of kin. But if he's here in our time on his own then I don't know who that'd be. A friend would be my closest bet — hopefully you or I." And then she added, thoughtfully, "how come you don't know about Porriduum anyway, Tom? Doesn't your home world send any of its prisoners there?" Tom nearly laughed out loud at the thought of it. If there was a deterrent anything like the notion of Porriduum back on Earth, he was sure there'd be much fewer crimes committed.

"No. My planet deals with its prisoners… independently," he managed.

"I don't know how they get away with that," Kayleesh scoffed. "One whole justice system confined to a single planet?"

"Well actually, there is more than one system in place. Different countries have different laws-"

"Well that's just absurd!" she interjected. The Augtopian thought for a moment, as though trying to rationalise the concept. Her violet eyes flickered their gaze around the room in deep ponder. She curled a golden lock of stray hair behind an elfin ear and concluded at last. "Hmm… well maybe the Milky Way galaxy doesn't come under the same ruling. Although it is technically a local galaxy."

"Maybe," Tom affirmed. Kayleesh seemed to accept this supposition. She looked Tom in the eye.

"I hope it wasn't my fault he got caught," she bit her lip. "It was my idea to grill him about his past. If someone had been listening when you were talking to him…"

"Exactly, it was me who was talking to him. I chose to question him. If it was anyone's fault it was mine," Tom argued.

"In fairness, it was Raphyl who originally brought up the subject —he didn't have to say anything, did he?" Tom's silence was his reply of agreement, despite the pair's genuine feelings of guilt. "Oh, I hope he contacts us soon."

As though he had extrasensory abilities, Raphyl's familiar tones emitted from Tom's timepiece.

"Hey, Tombo."

"Raphyl!" Tom exclaimed with surprise. "Where are you? What happened?" he asked excitedly, almost shouting.

"Relax, Tombo, I'm fine," came the lax response. "I'm on a ship. Pretty cool looking thing — could do with a going over with Mayty's cleaning device though." The volume of his voice fluctuated slightly as though he were looking around.

"You're on a prison-ship?" Kayleesh asked, impatiently. She knew they wouldn't allow Raphyl more time than was necessary for his final conversation.

"Is that you, Kayleesh? You're there too? Oh, hello," he said pleasantly, with all the urgency of a tortoise waking from hibernation.

"Hello Raphyl, yes it's me," she said through gritted teeth. "Just tell us how long you're going for."

"Fifty Porriduum days, they said," came the reply. A sigh followed.

"Fifty Porriduum days – how long is that?" Tom turned to Kayleesh. She dismissed his question with a brisk wave.

"We'll work that out later. Raphyl, what did they arrest you for?" her speech was more urgent now.

"I told Tom already I was hiding. But I didn't explain to him that I'm innocent."

"What is it they believe you've done, Raph?" Tom's heart was quickening by such a degree that he feared the timepiece's other function would activate and would respond to his raised stress levels and inappropriately set off its piercing distress signal. He tried to calm down, taking several deep breaths.

"They think… they think I'm a murderer, but they've got it wrong, Tom, they've got it wrong!" the strain in his voice was evident now, sobs of desperation finally breaking through his speech. If Raphyl was panicking, it was definitely time to start worrying.

"Murder?" Kayleesh echoed. "Who do they think you've murdered?"

"My parents," came the guarded response.

"Your parents?"

"But I didn't do it!"

"But… how could they get it wrong? The police never get it wrong." Kayleesh implored. Tom raised an eyebrow.

"They don't now; they have ways. But the police from my time —they must have followed me here somehow. They're different from modern Truxxian police."

"Why did you run to the future? How?" Tom demanded.

"Why? I suppose I panicked. I always thought I could get back —but I was wrong," he said tearfully. There was a gruff voice in the background which Tom understood to be a guard. "I've got to go now," Raphyl said in a low voice.

"What? But what do we do now? You've got to prove your innocence. We will prove your innocence," Kayleesh promised, impetuously.

"Bye guys." And then there was silence.

# CHAPTER 5

The Augtopian Kayleesh and the Earthling Tom Bowler gaped silently at each other for a full krom. The only sound was the soft hum of the apartment's stable enviro system. It was Tom who spoke first.

"How are we going to prove his innocence exactly?"

"We'll find out the facts, Tom. We need to piece it together."

"Why can't we just hijack one of TSS's Transit ships and rescue him?" Tom said, irritably.

"You know why, Tom. That'd be -"

"Impossible, I know," finished Tom. "I was joking. Besides, if we did steal a ship, we'd end up in Porriduum ourselves and what good would that do?"

"A ship might be a good start though," Kayleesh mused." Or at least someone with a ship — I'll contact Hyganty!" her violet eyes glinted excitedly.

"The praying mantis creature?" Tom blurted.

"The what?" Kayleesh looked confused. "The Submian, Tom," she corrected him.

"Whatever," Tom scowled. Why did she always have to feel she had to enlist the help of the bug-eyed monsters? Wasn't their small team capable enough of this duty? Maybe not, he pondered. Kayleesh mirrored his scowl and didn't dignify his nonsense with a reply.

Schlomm Putt rapped his fat fingers on the control desk of the Cluock's bridge. Why had he agreed on letting his foolish brother holiday on Radiakka? He couldn't trust Hannond to be alone for five kroms. Destroying their transnational flag? He could have at least been arrested for doing something worth-while — something which could lead to possible financial gain. Where was destroying a flag going to get him other than Porriduum and a bad name as a xenophobe? The Glorbian sighed. He supposed that he'd have to be the one to bail him out — no, no that would mean spending money.

He'd be the one to *break* him out. Unless he could intercept the prison-ship and get to him before he even got there. He could hijack the prison ship. He pondered. And be lumbered with a hundred or more murderers and thieves? He'd have to think this one through. He jumped down from his squat flight chair and lifted his timepiece to his mouth.

"Hannond, I'm coming to get you," he announced, then slapped his brow at his own stupidity. Hannond was now incommunicado, he remembered. He looked around the unnecessarily large ship and felt strangely empty. Perhaps he was hungry, he decided.

Tom was in the waiting room at the holoceiver exchange. He hadn't wanted to spend his wages on evenings out in bar Six Seven recently without his drinking partner and he hadn't been in the mood for spotoon, so Tom had saved some Ds and booked himself a session in this bizarre parody of a phone booth. He had no idea how his friends on Earth were going to help his situation, but he craved normality. Even fifteen minutes of it.

The waiting area was a clinical looking, uninspiring room lined with seated beings of all colour and race. Some were dressed in compsuits, others wore TSS uniforms and one or two sat conspicuously in their home world attire. He gazed at the receptionist behind the long desk. The same race as the holoceiver being itself, the psychic female yellow-transparent bubble bobbed around on her ergonomic seat which struggled as much as ever to make sense of the light viscosity of her frame. He watched a customer who was standing in front of the desk chat away to the faceless bubble calmly and without alarm. It appeared from Tom's point of view that she was ignoring the client although Tom knew different. He knew that when she conversed, her eerie voice simply bypassed the ears and planted its words in the listener's brain. He shuddered at the thought. He still wasn't comfortable with his half of the conversation being plucked from his mind almost before he could utter it.

It was soon Tom's turn to enter the holoceiver booth. The door shushed closed behind him. As he had done so before, but resisting the urge to grimace, he stepped inside the bubble creature which filled the booth as though he were stepping inside a man-shaped vehicle. His entire body was now encased inside the suit of yellow bubble armour. His vision had a yellow tint from the view through the being's skin. He confirmed where he wished to go and soon enough the view of the yellow-hazed bare interior of the booth transposed into the twilit bricked wall of his best friend's house. It was evening and Tom could hear the faint roar of an accelerating motorbike in the distance and the rush of the evening air about him. Familiarity. Tom instinctively pulled his arms around himself as if to shield his body from the wind, but he realised that his projected body was not able to feel the cold air or the fallen leaves which were encircling his feet. He looked up at the stars which were just twinkling into sight through the shepherd's delight purple sunset. He missed looking up at Earth's view of the stars.

He hoped that Nathan would soon appear as his holographic projection wasn't able to knock on the door. It was only his own house he was able to access unaided, through some peculiar system the holoceiver being used. He looked up at the windows of the semi-detached house – all the lights were off. Feeling foolish as he was wasting expensive time standing around on his friend's driveway, he looked down at his holographic feet which were projected convincingly on the tarmac. He sighed. His frown soon transformed into a wide grin, however, as he heard a familiar voice cry out in surprise.

"Hey, bud!" Nathan, dark haired and scruffy looking, was sauntering up the driveway. He was smiling and carrying a blue carrier bag which was clinking with bottles. "Want to join me for a Star Wars marathon and a bevvie?"

"I wish I had the time and the means," Tom opened his arms in a shrug to indicate his lack of corporeal existence.

"I'll have to drink them all myself then," Nathan laughed. "So, what's this visit in aid of?" he asked parenthetically, fumbling in his pocket for his house key. He let himself and the hologram of his friend into the empty house. Tom shrugged. Images of the Porriduum Kayleesh had described to him flooded into his mind. He felt so helpless about Raphyl's exile to the prison planet. He didn't know what he was doing here in the Truxxian's time of need and didn't expect Nathan to understand half of it.

He smiled to himself. With all that Tom had been through, here was his childhood friend, still here in this small town. He was still going to the same local shop for beer, carried home in the same inadequate, thin blue carrier bags. Normality. Tom followed Nathan through to the kitchen where he placed three bottles into the fridge and proceeded to open the fourth with the bottle opener on his key chain. Tom noticed that the fridge looked very different to how it normally did. Instead of the usual harvest of organic crops, the shelves were inhabited by plastic cartons. There was a hunk of cheese, a packet of butter, and a stack of leaking Tupperware boxes. Tom looked at his friend who had seemed so happy by his arrival. There was a hint of concern in his expression as he swigged from his bottle. He looked more closely around the kitchen. There were plates in the sink with grease so thick and dried on that Tom doubted a pneumatic drill would penetrate through. The bin was apocalyptically overflowing – there was barely a free space to stand. None of this would have mattered to Tom had he not remembered this house to be anything but the complete opposite; the pristine home he had visited since he was a child.

"Er… Nathan," he ventured. "Everything's… OK isn't it?" Nathan drew the bottle away from his mouth, slowly.

"Er… yeah, yeah. Well, no, bud. My er… my mum's in hospital." He took a quick swig in an attempt to disguise his discomfort.

"Ah. Right. How come?"

"You know how she's always rushing around doing ten things at once? Running her own business, obsessively cleaning the house, looking after me and dad…" Tom nodded. "Well… she… she had a nervous breakdown."

"Woah." Tom didn't know what to say. "And she's in hospital?"

"Er, yeah," Nathan coughed nervously. "Dad signed the papers two weeks ago."

It was then that Tom realised what kind of hospital Nathan meant.

"Ironic really, eh?" Nathan laughed thinly and waved a hand, gesticulating the chaotic state of the uncharacteristically grubby room. Tom gave what he hoped was an understanding smile. It seemed things weren't so normal here after all. Nathan had his own problems. "So —how are things in outer space?" Nathan grinned, leading Tom though to the living room. The lounge was in a slightly less repellent state although it still felt as though Tom had walked into the wrong house. He was only glad he couldn't smell it. "Still exciting?"

"You could say that," said Tom. He had considered not telling him his problems in light of the situation, but perhaps Nathan needed something else to think about. In the same way he had. Tom explained as best he could as much as he knew about Raphyl's imminent fate from what Kayleesh had told him. Exaggerating here and there as people do in an attempt to make their stories as grandiose and impressive as possible, Tom divulged. "And so, I thought I'd pay my best bud a visit as he's usually quite good at coming up with clever plans," he finished. Nathan's eyes widened. He rested his spent bottle on the already cluttered carpet.

"Me?" He belched and gave his own chest two light thumps. "I think this one's beyond me, space boy."

Tom sighed, despite having not really expected any other response. However, as he looked at his friend, he could almost see the cogs working behind his eyes. His face was screwing up in thought.

"I'll have a think, bud. It'll be a good distraction." He gave a genuine grin. "Are you calling in on your folks this time?"

Tom shook his head. "No, I don't have time. A five-minute visit all the way from Exeter to the Midlands won't seem plausible a second time."

"True, but I doubt the first thing they'll suspect is that you're actually a hologram of their son being beamed down from a distant planet. That sounds even less plausible." Tom laughed and Nathan joined in. The sound of the laughter seemed to be fading, however, as was his vision. The yellow hue of the psychic bubble holoceiver being was becoming apparent once more.

"Looks like my time's up," Tom's face fell. His hologram was beginning to lose its validity, his presence in the suburban living room waning. The yellow-tinged Nathan seemed to notice this too. He lifted his hand by way of a wave.

"See ya, bud."

Moments later, Tom's consciousness was back with his real body in a holoceiver booth on planet Truxxe. He stepped out through the transparent creature's skin.

# CHAPTER 6

"I know conditions are not ideal with Raphyl's temporary absence, but do your best, team." Tom's supervisor robot Miss Lolah articulated with her beautiful, digitised feminine voice. Tom was grinning inanely at her and gazing at the speaker which jutted out underneath her camera lens eye. Miss Lolah was a pherobot which meant that her bronze, graceless, body emitted a pheromone field which entranced male staff members and employed popular method of control on Truxxe. It was arguably a sexist, outdated and somewhat disturbing system, but it was popular throughout the northern hemisphere, all the same. Clunking her way across the restaurant, the male workers of the Express Cuisine were rapt in her every movement. They abided by a pherobot's every instruction, fell over themselves to comply, worked with immense enthusiasm... then felt the foolish after-sensation on her departure from the vicinity.

Miss Lolah disappeared into the staff room, content that her workforce was sufficiently motivated for the time being. Kayleesh shook her head at this usual pathetic performance and, full of her own natural fervour for work, began to tap her authorisation code into the till.

Tom and Kayleesh worked hard at the Express Cuisine that day, their friend's plight lying heavy in their minds. They got through the breakfast rush and the lunch time rush and the post mid-sun munchies and tried to focus their thoughts on their job. But how could Tom continue to work as though Raphyl no longer existed? He wasn't off sick or malingering out of choice, their friend was in *trouble* and he needed them.

At one of the quieter moments just after lunch, Tom recognised the green insectile creature that entered the restaurant. It was Hyganty. Apparently wearing a Charlatans hoody and jeans stretched ridiculously over his skeletal-looking frame, the Submian approached the counter.

"I hear you're after a spaceship?" he directed his question at Kayleesh who ran quickly over to meet him.

"Ssh… keep it down," she raised a finger to her lips. "What happened to being a conspiracy theorist?"

"But why all the secrecy?" Hyganty asked in hushed tones. "There's nothing iniquitous about riding in a spacecraft." Kayleesh looked around her, leaned over the counter and whispered.

"There is if you're doing it in work's time!"

"Hmm… then it seems as though this little adventure you have planned may take longer than I imagined," the Submian pondered. "Perhaps you should tell me what it is exactly that you propose to do." Kayleesh explained Raphyl's plight to Hyganty while Tom served the trickle of punters. He could hear their hushed voices and see Hyganty nodding now and then in comprehension. Why did she always have to conspire with him? What was it with her? Perhaps the availability of the Submian ship was just an excuse. Tom could never elude his jealousy when Hyganty was around Kayleesh, even if his suspicions had proved groundless. Several minutes later the two approached him. Like a couple, Tom thought.

"So, are you two planning on flying out to Porriduum to rescue Raphyl?" Tom asked, somewhat irritably.

"No, well… nothing that adventurous yet," Hyganty replied. "There's a lot of research we need to do first. We need to find out why Raphyl escaped to our time, how he did it and what really happened to his parents."

"I think we should start by searching his room," Kayleesh said, simply.

"Kayleesh, if he was on the run, I doubt he'd be stupid enough to leave anything lying around his room which would give anything away," Tom protested. He threw down his cloth. Kayleesh gave a half shrug.

"Well, it's a start. I have a spare key to his apartment – he's always locking himself out. You know how vigilant he isn't."

"Well as we're Raphyl's only hope of ever getting out of that place, so I suppose we should start as soon as possible. We should have a nose round his apartment after work," Tom suggested.

"Exactly — we should start tonight. And we're not being nosy, Tom. We're *investigating*. It's completely different!"

Tom and Kayleesh met Hyganty in the foyer at ten kroms past the sixth hour. They made their way to the lifts and Kayleesh pushed the circular button on the wall adjacent to the nearest lift. The door hummed open and the three stepped into the pristine interior of the capacious compartment. The Augtopian manipulated the track-ball controls on the wall and lined the arrow up so that it pointed to thirty-two on the ring of gold numbers. This was the floor of the immense building where most of the employees resided. The lift lurched upwards and soon arrived at its destination. The door purred open and they progressed along the long corridor, the perspective of which would have put Johannes Vermeer to shame.

Tom almost routinely stopped when he reached his own door, but the small party continued past it and he realised that he had not yet been as far as Raphyl's quarters. They passed room forty-two where Guy Hasprin lived and Kayleesh stopped outside number sixty-seven. The number, which was being translated by the compound's ALSID system, was printed in blue lettering half-way up the door. She casually disclosed a key from her robe pocket and turned it in the lock. On entering, Tom's mind instantly flashed back to the sorry state of what his friend Nathan's home had become. This apartment near mirrored it with its chaotic clutter. Again, mess itself did not bother Tom, but he didn't welcome the idea of sifting through the unpalatable jumble sale of possessions for clues. He sighed as he scanned his eyes across the landscape of accumulated articles.

"I didn't realise he had so much... stuff!" Tom exclaimed, kneeling down and half-heartedly leafing through a pile of threadbare compsuits. "How long has Raphyl been living at TSS?"

"Well I've worked with him for about two years, so at least that long," Kayleesh replied, searching inquisitively through a knapsack. She didn't seem to have any shame in doing so.

Tom, however, felt more than a little uncomfortable in looking through his friend's possessions. He wasn't sure he'd like Kayleesh trawling through his belongings had it been he who had been deported.

"And how long is a year on Truxxe?"

"Well Truxxe doesn't orbit a sun, as you know, but a year is calculated at four hundred rotations."

"Nice round number," smiled Tom. Something shiny caught his eye. It was a large pile of silver-coated plastic cards. Tom splayed a selection of them out in his hands like a deck of playing cards. There was hand-written text at the top of each card. They seemed to be song titles and band names, albeit obscure ones. There was also a blank one. He picked up still more of them and noticed that buried underneath the pile was a stack of paper.

"What's that you've found, Tom?" Hyganty's globular eyes rested curiously on the papers in Tom's hands.

"Oh, I don't know. Some documents of some kind, letters, flyers, newspapers," Tom said casually.

"Anything of interest?" Did he expect Tom to pry through the whole pile? Shrugging, he handed Hyganty half of the jumbled heap for his own perusal. But he soon regretted the move as he should have guessed that Hyganty would have to be the hero. Why did he hand him the evidence on a silver platter? For there, right on the top of the pile was the first step in the direction of solving the truth of Raphyl's past.

"So Raphyl has been accused of murdering his parents?" Hyganty waved the letter triumphantly — a heroic flag. "Here are their names — Truxxians Raghael and Mirrie and their son Raphyl — no surnames of course, being Truxxians. It seems that at one time they won an award of some kind. They were both architects apparently." It was a news article. Tom took a closer look. There was a photograph of two Truxxian adults, the smaller one cradling the then baby Raphyl in her long arms.

"That's great, Hyganty, well done!" Kayleesh beamed. Tom opened his mouth to protest - *he* had found the papers after all. But he stopped himself — Kayleesh didn't care who had found it. Besides, he might find something even more helpful. "What else does it say, Hyganty?"

"Let's see." Hyganty murmured, incoherently, as he scanned through the article. "Ah, it says that the couple were originally from the South but settled down to start a family in the East. That's where they created their company ACD, Authority Construction Designs. At ACD they used their combined talents to help design various important structures throughout the neighbouring galaxies. Their award was for their design of the Parliamentary Building in the capital of Wheyland on Radiakka. They also…"

"OK Hyganty, I think the rest is probably irrelevant," interrupted Kayleesh, not unkindly. "So now we know where Raphyl and his parents are from, at least."

"And when!" Hyganty pointed out. "This article was written over three hundred years ago!"

"So Raphyl's travelled three hundred years into his future?" Tom gasped. "But how?" Kayleesh shook her head slowly.

"I… I don't know. Oh, I wish Raphyl had had time to explain to us how he got here." Tom asked the question which had been burning inside him. He hoped Kayleesh and the stony-faced Submian wouldn't laugh at him.

"Are there time machines… have you ever heard of people actually travelling through time?"

"You mean like in fiction?" A loud laugh erupted from her. "No, of course not!"

Tom shrugged. Do aliens read sci-fi? He wondered.

"But there is a possibility he was in cryo-state for all that time. It's technically a form of time travel. One-way of course," Hyganty piped up.

"You mean he was frozen for *three hundred years?*" Tom raised his eyebrows.

"It's certainly a possibility. Experiments with such technology were being conducted then after all. How else could it be explained? The date is on the newspaper article. He must have got here somehow."

"Raphyl said he was on the run — a time fugitive," said Kayleesh. "He must have known about the technology — even way back then. I wouldn't have credited Raphyl with the intellect to use it as a means of escape though. I mean, no offence to him, but he's not the most quick-witted amongst us, you have to admit."

"True. But there are two things which might equate for that," Hyganty said knowingly, a pincer resting thoughtfully on his chin. All he needs now is a pipe and a deerstalker hat, thought Tom. "Firstly, it is likely that Raphyl made this decision in a panic; the opportunity revealed itself and he took it. Secondly, the reason that cryogenics is no longer used is its effect on the brain."

"What are you saying? That the Raphyl we know is not the same as the Raphyl who lived back then? That his intellect has altered?" Kayleesh shrieked.

"I'm saying there is a likelihood. I'm sure that he's essentially the same boy who was frozen, but after three hundred years there would have been a degree of brain-cell loss. I am not equipped with the knowledge of such antiquated technology, but unless there was some kind of safety precaution then there must have been a significant level of risk involved."

"Well, it would certainly explain a few things!" Kayleesh gave a light-hearted chuckle. "So, do you think that when they finally found his body in cryo, they followed him?"

"Who knows? They may have risked that, or they may have waited."

"Waited? This long? Then why didn't they arrest him when he thawed out? Why didn't they guard the capsule?"

"I don't know all the answers, Kayleesh, I am merely speculating. Maybe it wasn't that simple."

Tom's head was buzzing with thoughts of what Raphyl might have been like before being frozen and how he had escaped as he continued searching around his friend's belongings. Maybe he'd find something else from Raphyl's past. But other than meaningless papers, receipts, empty food cartons, clothes and magazines, the three found nothing which they deemed relevant. Kayleesh eventually suggested they leave with the evidence they had. Hyganty and Tom agreed.

Although Tom lingered behind and selected an assortment of the silver cards at random. *I'm only borrowing them, Raphyl. I'll bring them back tomorrow.* The cards seemed to be just the right dimensions for the slot in his melody mech.

Nathan was wondering whether things would get any worse for him. His best friend had left for planets new; his mum had practically added a strait jacket to the top of her wardrobe list, and his dad was grumpier than ever. Even Max hadn't been as much fun since his cousin Tom had left. It just wasn't the same. Nothing was the same. Searching fruitlessly around the kitchen for a clean cup, he noticed something at the edge of his vision, a bright light outside the window. Nathan gasped.

# CHAPTER 7

*If you're planning to intercept the ship, Schlomm, you're running out of time,* Hannond thought to himself. They were moving. At least, he thought they were. The ship's engines were noisy whether stationary or in motion, but Hannond Putt had gathered from the dialogue he had heard on the other side of his holding cell door that their arrival was imminent. He looked at his half-eaten breakfast with dismay and hoped that the chefs on Porriduum were superior to the ones on the prison transporter ship.

Tom Bowler grinned as the first piece of music to be heard in his apartment since his arrival, sprang from the sleek melody mech on his living room wall. There was the sound of a female vocalist against an accompaniment of what sounded like electric strings, a deep percussion instrument and androgynous backing vocals. The lyrics bordered on teenage angst, although the lines scanned terribly as they translated through the ALSID system and so nothing rhymed. Tom found it highly amusing. He listened again, this time pressing the diamond-shaped button on the side of the unit as Raphyl had explained to him. Once it had played through, Tom ejected the silver card, took the blank one from his pocket, inserted it into the same slot and pressed the diamond button again. A short pause, a soft click, and the angry vocalist began her rants about bad parenting once again.

Copy successful! A cheery message appeared on the unit's small display. Smiling confidently to himself, he proceeded to go through the remains of Raphyl's already duplicated music collection in the same manner until the copy card bleeped to indicate its satiation.

The following rotation, Hasprin's Legion had a Spotoon game at BB's favourite recreational place, Oxxo's Bar. The place was unfamiliar to him and he was more than a little apprehensive, but Tom had decided to play anyway. He would have the support of his team-mates and he didn't want to give BB's leader Baff Bulken an excuse to disparage him further in his absence. He allowed himself these few hours with his team during which he could take his mind off Raphyl's predicament, before he met up with Kayleesh to discuss their next move. Raphyl wasn't going anywhere.

He took the lift to the recreational level where he found Ransel and Chazner, the Truxxian players from his team.

"Hi, Tom," Chazner grinned at him. They both tilted their heads at Tom, their right ears pointing in his direction, waggling. Tom returned the gesture, minus the waggle, glad that he didn't have to enter the devil's lair alone.

A broken red hologram above a double door fizzed intermittently in and out of existence, inaccurately asserting that they were about to enter "xo's ar". The doors ground open noisily and they entered a room half the size of bar Six Seven and with a quarter of the appeal. The grubby interior was in stark contrast to the pristine corridor, as though in an act of sheer rebellion. The room was softly lit, though this fact suggested the function of concealment rather than an attempt to create an agreeable ambiance. The room was overcrowded and the atmosphere, oppressive. The music differed from that played in bar Six Seven although Tom could place the genre no more easily. It formed a feeling in his ears more uncomfortable than wax build up and Tom wiggled a finger around in both ears, irritably.

The barman looked like the grumpy cousin of Lan, the barman to whom Tom had become accustomed. He felt as though he had stepped into a parallel universe. Sneering at him from behind the bar, a caged wild beast, the barman simply raised his bedraggled monobrow, quizzically. Tom tentatively ordered drinks for the three of them. As soon as his beverage was placed on the dusty counter, he picked it up again and took a large gulp. Ransel and Chazner took nervous sips of their own drinks and the three outsiders shied away from the bar. They were soon joined by Mayty Reeston and Ghy Hasprin, the remainder of their team, who strode in with their usual air of confidence.

Mayty was sporting his usual absurdly wide grin which inhabited much of his round, orange face and the Herculean Ghy seemed to be scanning the room for the opposition who had evidently not yet arrived. The five of them presented their team greeting in unison.

Tom was just finishing his drink when Ghy nodded in the direction of the double-doors. The opposition had arrived. The monstrously built Baff Bulken glowered menacingly at Hasprin's Legion, yellow saliva already formulating on his lower lip. Muscular and weighty, the green colossus led his motley crew into the room. Why had Ghy agreed to this match? Did he want his team to end up in hospital again? Tom peered over his glass as the BBs rambled towards the Spotoon board. He recognised the team members from the Big Match several weeks ago. He smirked at the memory of their being disqualified for unfair play; Hasprin's Legion had won that round by default. But there was one team member he recognised even more so.

It couldn't be!

What was Nathan doing with the BB's?

*What was Nathan doing on Truxxe?!*

# CHAPTER 8

Tom Bowler blinked. No, his eyes were not misleading him. And he was sober. There, standing mere metres away in the roughest alien bar in the universe was his lifelong friend Nathan Reed. Speechless, Tom stared; utterly astounded at the presence of the only other Earthling in the room. And he appeared to be socialising with his enemies. What was he *doing* here? He stared as Nathan casually fired some preliminary test spit balls at the Spotoon board — rather accurately. No, no, no this was Tom's sport, it was Tom's adventure. This couldn't be happening — and Nathan was on the opposition's team. This was all wrong. What was happening? He knew he should have been happy to see his friend there — on this world which he had described to Nathan through the holoceiver — but his resounding reaction was sheer confusion.

Nathan still hadn't spotted him, and Tom continued to stare fixedly over the rim of his glass. Suddenly, a heavy, clammy hand gripped his shoulder, but Tom resisted the urge to turn around and kept his fellow human in sight.

"Everything all right, Tom?" Ghy Hasprin asked him. "Stop worrying, there are plenty of witnesses here. I'm sure it'll be a good, clean game — no fights this time." He chuckled.

"What? Oh, right, yeah," Tom said, somewhat distractedly. "Ghy, that new team member —"

"The human?" Ghy interrupted. "Looks like the dribblers finally got what they wanted. Bulken was envious when we enlisted you and now it looks like they've dumped one of their team-mates for a human competitor." His gaze still on Nathan, half expecting that the apparition would vanish if he looked away, Tom made his way over to his friend. Ignoring the raspy, hot breath of Bulken and the contemptuous snarls and hisses of the other BBs, he squeezed his way through the crowded room. Nathan looked as though he was wearing a second-hand compsuit for the motif on the front was faded and the knees of the lower half were slightly torn. Tom called out his name. Nathan looked startled.

"Tom?" Nathan left the side of his new play mates and strolled over to him. "What are you doing here?"

"What am I-? Nathan — how the hell did you get to Truxxe? And more importantly — what are you doing on *their* team?" he added distastefully. He wasn't sure which answer he craved more urgently. Nathan simply grinned at him.

"Cool, eh? Baff asked me to join his team earlier today — apparently, I should be exceptional at the sport, being a human and everything. I remembered you going on about Spotoon and I thought; why not?" He ran a hand through his dishevelled hair. "You're not on *their* team, are you?" he nodded in the direction of Hasprin's Legion.

"Hey, yes, that is my team!" Tom exclaimed, defensively. He shook his head in disbelief. "I'm sorry, I can't deal with this," Tom drank the dregs from his glass in one final swig and grabbed Nathan's compsuit by the hood.

"Come on, I think you've got a few things to explain." And he led Nathan out of the bar.

Tom didn't know where he was taking him, he just wanted to get out of *xo's ar*. He wanted answers. He wasn't sure which was his reigning emotion; fear, confusion, anger — all three bidding for top place in his aching skull.

"OK, from the beginning," Tom said, finally. They were walking aimlessly around the warren of passageways on the recreational level. "What happened?"

"It's weird seeing you here, Tom — weird actually being here in fact. I never imagined TSS to be so big!"

"Nathan!" Tom pleaded, resisting the urge to thump him.

"OK, OK. This is what happened. Wow, it all feels so much like a dream." He took a deep breath. "Well, I was at home in the kitchen, making myself a cheese and pickle sandwich, when I noticed a bright light outside the window. It was too bright to be car headlamps or anything like that. I was intrigued, so I went out of the back door to see what it was. You know how enclosed our back garden is? There's no way in is there? Anyway, I could see this glowing, this white light pulsing behind the apple trees. I went towards it. At first I thought it was you, bud. I thought you'd saved up your wages or won some space money and bought a ship and come back home in it. And then I saw that it *was* a ship. But when I didn't see you come out of it, I panicked. It was only a pod — I bet it was no bigger than my mum's people carrier. Anyway, the white light grew dim and so I could see a bit better and then I could make out two short men drawing near me. They were carrying weapons and their faces were grey with dark, almond-shaped eyes."

"Now, come on," Tom disputed. "I'm being serious. How did you really get here? Don't make out you were abducted by Greys from a fifties B movie, bud. It's just not like that,"

"Hey, I'm *here* aren't I? I'm not lying. You don't own the rights to interstellar travel!" Nathan scowled at Tom's disparagement. "Just listen, will you? In fact, it might explain where those sorts of stories come from." Tom shrugged and let his friend continue. "So, these two characters approached me, and they seemed to be looking at me with such serious expressions. Not hostile exactly, just kind of… stern. Anyway, their weapons were pointing in my direction the entire time, so I didn't protest when they each took one of my arms and began escorting me to the pod. They said that I had to be questioned. Something about a Truxxian named Raphyl — your colleague I believe, bud!" he said reproachfully, although his grin softened his tone.

"Raphyl? But how would you know anything about Raphyl's case?"

"Well I don't, but they knew that someone from Truxxe had been talking to me about it. Do you think the holoceiver you used must have been bugged?"

"I think it's simpler than that," Tom gulped. "The holoceivers are alive remember — and telepathic. It must have recorded the gist of the conversation somehow. I knew I couldn't trust my thoughts with those things." Tom scowled. "I wonder why they didn't take *me* for questioning?"

"It's probably only a matter of time," Nathan mused.

"So, what are you doing playing Spotoon if you're supposed to be under the charge of the Greys?"

"Well I thought, as I'm here, why not make the most of it? They will come and find me when they need me, I'm sure. They made me wear this," Nathan proffered his arm. An amber coloured bracelet encircled his left wrist. "Anyway, so they accompanied me to their pod, and I kept thinking how exciting it was. I needed a good excuse to get out of the house and that… situation… and there, literally on my doorstep, was a way out. And of all the planets I could have been taken to via abduction — I get taken to the same one as you!" He laughed at the idea of it.

"Well it's not that much of a coincidence, seeing as it's my fault," Tom reasoned.

"Don't feel bad about it, bud. This is the most exciting thing that's ever happened to me. I needed some escapism and man, I sure got it! The timing could not have been better. Their ship was so small. It smelled like the interior of a new car — all flashing lights and comfortable seats. My abductors were very quiet on the way here — in fact I don't remember the journey. I remember being given a drink —some green, warm fizzy stuff — and then I must have fallen asleep, because the next thing I knew we had docked. I must have missed the entire flight! Such a waste when you think about it. I'll bet they do that with all their abductees — drug them, take them off somewhere then return them. That's why no one in those UFO documentaries can ever remember the full story."

"Possibly. So, have they asked you any questions yet?"

"Not really. And I don't have much to tell them, anyway do I? The creatures who brought me here said that the chief who needs to speak to me isn't available at the moment — so I'm here."

"Right. So, where are you staying while you're here?"

"I don't know… a cell probably."

"A cell?" Tom gasped.

"Well, you don't expect them to put me up in the penthouse suite do you?"

"No, I suppose not," Tom shrugged.

"Hey, it can't be any worse than the state of my room at the moment, bud," he smiled bravely.

"There you are!" Ghy had caught up with them. He was smiling, but an anxious sigh betrayed him. "Come, on, we can't start the game without you two." Tom looked at Nathan, then at Ghy and shrugged. The three returned to Oxxo's Bar.

As the third round came to a close, BBs having won the decider, Kayleesh's silhouette appeared in the doorway. Grateful for an excuse to be out of the company of Baff Bulken's sweaty squad, Tom went to meet her.

"Can we talk somewhere else?" Kayleesh wrinkled her pixie-like nose in distaste. Tom noticed that her feet remained solidly on the corridor side of the entrance.

"Of course, I'll be back in a moment. There's someone I'd like you to meet." Tom promptly slipped back through the crowd, gave a half-hearted salute to his team and yelled for Nathan to follow him. Once outside the bar, Tom introduced the two.

"Oh, you're a human too?" Kayleesh smiled. Nathan laughed and nodded at this remark and held out his hand. Kayleesh eventually comprehended this alien gesture and gave it a delicate shake. "I'm from Augtopia. I work in the Express Cuisine restaurant with Tom and Raphyl. Or I did, until… Raphyl…" her face fell. She then added brightly, "come on, shall we all go and sit in bar Six Seven while there's still some evening left? We've got to plan our next move."

Feeling much more comfortable on familiar territory, Tom sat back in an ergonomic chair at a table situated in the corner of bar Six Seven. He felt deeply tranquil after being so utterly on edge in the previous establishment. He had his back to the wall, for one thing, and didn't have to keep spinning around like a deranged top, in case a BB fan decided to assault him. He chortled as Nathan sank into the seat next to him, the look of horror mixed with realisation on his face which Tom also must also have worn, the first time he had used one of these universal chairs.

"What's so funny, bud?" Nathan threw him a glance. They both laughed. "Hmm… this is so relaxing!"
Kayleesh smiled.
"I've had an idea of how to get to Raphyl."

# CHAPTER 9

Schlomm Putt's grin stretched across his face like a crack in a great boulder. He smugly steered the Cluock out of the docking bay of the Grayuuk and headed out into the void of space. Cloaking devices like the one with which he had just upgraded the Cluock were illegal, but his confidence in his crime overrode his cares. The crew on board the Grayuuk had equipped his beloved craft with the latest in ship stealth technology. The Glorbian's wallet was now lighter than a helium-filled holoceiver, but successfully executing the task of releasing Hannond from Porriduum's cells was only the first step. He would get his money back tenfold with his ship's modification; a dozen schemes were already being formed by his malevolent intellect.

The device was called a compositer, which used perception-altering technology which was analogous to the Wardrobian affect. Instead of altering the visualisation of clothing, it altered the observer's perception of an entire spaceship. This grand-scale deception device required an immense amount of energy from the source, so Schlomm's first stop was to refuel the Cluock at TSS.

Schlomm had decided to power down the compositer until he was nearer the prison planet. There was little need to disguise his meat-delivery ship at this stage, particularly as his company was a recognised supplier to the Truxxian service station. Happenstance had it that the Express Cuisine had placed an order with him mere hours ago so the opportunity to collect payment for the meat delivery at the same time made him grin even wider. The bonus was that the customer would be pleased at his prompt response to their order, although of course Schlomm didn't consider the feelings of anyone but Schlomm, and so this fact was superfluous.

The Glorbian cruised the ship through the silence of space, across the empty light years between Andromeda and Triangulum where he located the isolated planetoid Truxxe. As he neared, the bright lights of the vast service station shone beacon-like, a lighthouse on the perpetually dark landscape of the world. The welcoming glow of the complex intensified as he brought the ship down and into the station's immense freight bay. The stubby creature jumped down from his flight chair onto his flat feet and before he could descend the Cluock's ramp to make his presence known, he was surprised to find a TSS employee already driving up on a hovering fork-lift truck.

Once the transaction was complete, with a fist-full of Ds, Schlomm negotiated the Cluock to the ship's specific refuelling station and barked orders for the tank to be filled to the brim.

Some hours later, the Cluock reached Porriduum space. Nearing the edge of the Triangulum galaxy, the ship's scanner detected a fleet of prison transporter ships. Schlomm's heart was thumping a war-dance in his chest as his itchy fingers crept menacingly towards the shiny new compositer activation controls. Taking a deep breath, he knew that if he didn't initiate the device soon, his ship would be identified, and he would be on his way to Porriduum in less favourable circumstances. Would his plan work? Aboard the Grayuuk, he had been convinced that his ship would have a remarkable resemblance to any ship it attempted to imitate.

His eyes tight shut, baring his teeth, Schlomm blindly brought his hand down on the switch. No sound. He slowly opened his eyes, unpeeled his hand from the controls and heard nothing but the hum of the engines accompanied by the war-dance in his chest. He had expected there to be an audible indication that the device was operational, some sort of fanfare perhaps. Maybe there was a visual clue. Scanning the systems and monitors, Schlomm eyed every visual apparatus available; nothing. Panicking, not knowing whether the compositer was working, he grabbed hold of the flight controls, and proceeded to pull the ship back round in the opposite direction.

"Considering how much money I spent on it, they could have at least fitted a flashing LED to the controls to let me know if the thing's working!" he grumbled to himself.

"Ship five five seven," a voice boomed through his ship's ALSID speaker. It was so unexpected that Schlomm almost fell over in fright. "Come in, five five seven," it came again.

"Er… ship five five seven responding," Schlomm replied in what he hoped turned out to be a confident manner.

"Why are you turning away? Proceed to Porriduum. Repeat, proceed to Porriduum. The window is closing."

It had worked! The other prison ships must have expected to see ship five five seven and therefore had mistaken the cloaked Cluock as that very ship. Smugger than ever, wondering how he had ever doubted the ingenious device, Schlomm steered the meat delivery ship cum prisoner transporter back round to face Porriduum. As he approached, other prison ships neared, following the same course. A thought struck him. How was he going to explain arriving at a prison planet without any prisoners?

"What's your plan?" Tom asked, excitedly.

"Well it's not a fully-fledged plan exactly — but it is an idea. Although I'm not sure you're going to like it," said Kayleesh.

"Go on," Tom sighed.

"Well, while we wait for Hyganty to get back to us about borrowing a ship, I was thinking — you know how you came to live on Truxxe by getting a job here? Well, so did I now I come to think of it – anyway, I was thinking more specifically of you, Tom. What I'm trying to get at is… well… you don't fancy a change of career do you?" Kayleesh asked, apprehensively. Tom's eyes widened.

"Are you suggesting what I think you're suggesting? You want to me apply for a job on Porriduum to get to Raphyl? Are you crazy?"

It was all Nathan could do to stop himself from spurting a mouthful of Truxxian beer across the table in surprise. "I have to agree with Tom on this one. From what I've heard, Porriduum is not somewhere I'd want to work!"

Kayleesh gave an apologetic half-shrug.

"It wouldn't be the same as being incarcerated there," she offered.

"Maybe not but come on. Anyway, why would they let a burger boy work as a prison officer?" Tom pointed out. Kayleesh gave him one of her sweet smiles.

"Not as a prison officer, silly. They do feed the prisoners on Porriduum you know — they need burger boys there too. Or porridge boys at least!" her smile broke into a stifled giggle. Neither human shared her mirth.

"I still don't see how it's going to work — even if for some stupid reason I agreed to this — I still wouldn't be able to get near to Raphyl, least of all smuggle him back in my suitcase on a Friday… er… on the last day of my working week. We don't know anything about the structure of the prison inside the planet, we don't know enough about their security system… there are far too many unknowns and far too much security." How could she seriously propose this absurd scheme?

"Well maybe you won't have to smuggle him out. Maybe you can find a way of proving his innocence! Get some information from him when you serve him his supper — anything that might help towards his case. I told you it wasn't exactly the Glorbian Fawkensday Plot, but you have to admit that you'd have more of a clue from that standpoint than from all the way out here on Truxxe. I just feel so powerless here, Tom. We need someone on the inside."

"Our whole problem is that one of us is inside!" Tom ricocheted. Beer snorted out of Nathan's nose and he brought his hand to his sodden mouth, chortling.

"Good one, Tom. You have to admit the girl has a point though —there's only so much we can do from this side of the barbed fence. Or neutron star, as it were."

"You won't be laughing if the police decide to banish you to Porriduum, Nathan. You're not in the clear yet." Tom jabbed at the tag around Nathan's wrist. Nathan gave his friend's arm a punch in return. "Maybe they're not advertising for staff at the moment," Tom said, hopefully.

"I wouldn't worry about that, they have a faster employee turnover than the TSS Sewers," Kayleesh said with an annoying amount of confidence. "I don't want to push you Tom, but what do you think of the idea?"

"Of your half an idea? I suppose it's a start. And it might accomplish more than sifting through more of Raphyl's junk and crossing our fingers." And the smile that Kayleesh gave him at that moment was almost worth the prospect of what might lay ahead of him. Almost.

## CHAPTER 10

The next evening, Kayleesh and Nathan accompanied Tom to Truxxe's equivalent of the Job Centre. There was a branch at the service station, but the jobs on offer there were specifically for TSS employment. Tom was glad for a reason to get out of the complex for a while. He was beginning to feel a little claustrophobic, which he then felt guilty about, given how Raphyl must be feeling in his cell.

Nathan watched with obvious fascination as Kayleesh casually booked out an ALSID bot, which they proceeded to take out into the darkness of Truxxe. The translation unit glowed obediently amongst the small group as the bright environment of the service station faded with every footfall, as did the station's Wardrobian Effect. Soon the only light around them was being emitted from the ALSID bot and the occasional light rocks which dotted their path.

Tom had only ever ventured outside of the complex once before on foot. He was amazed once more at the contrast between the constant dazzling hubbub of the station and the everlasting dark silence of the wilderness. He couldn't fathom how Kayleesh knew where she was going. They seemed to be travelling in the same direction as Raphyl had taken him to the Crossvein Visitor Centre, but the terrain was markedly different. It was as though they were walking on a blanket of moss. The ALSID bot seemed better equipped to cope with travelling over the spongy ground and Tom found himself having to watch his step to avoid slipping over into the yellowing, sun-starved slime.

"I hope we don't bump into Tyrander," Tom thought aloud. "He wouldn't be pleased if his employees were found job hunting, would he?"

"I can't see him willingly walking around out here," Kayleesh shrugged. "He'd more likely be in TSS's own Job Selector anyway or contacting ones further afield — like the one you used."

Tom reflected on the day he had seen the advertisement for the job at TSS. If he had known where that application would have led him, he would not have believed it. As a child he had always dreamed of far off worlds. Now he wished he could take in the beauty of this planet, his new home. Looking around him he felt liberated to be outside after living exclusively inside the complex for the past few weeks, but his freedom was a still a little curbed, here, in the progressing pool of light. If he strained his eyes, he could make out one or two light-rocks, but they were becoming scarce now. Tom still half-expected that should he wait long enough; the sun would rise, and he would see the mish-mash landscape of Truxxe in its full glory. But the sun never rose on Truxxe, and that thought saddened him. The warm core of the planet ensured their journey was not a cold one and he was comfortable inside his compsuit, but sometimes he missed the sensation of sun rays on his back and the warm scent of summer or a crisp winter morning. He hadn't noticed before how important passing of the seasons were in a person's life. He would have laughed at the very thought of longing for rain, wind, anything other than the continuous status quo of the artificial environment of TSS.

Just when Tom thought his ankles were going to give way from constantly righting himself on the soft, uneven ground, they finally crossed over onto stony terrain. Their footsteps crunched now on the hard ground, after the silence of the damp moss. Kayleesh lugged the ALSID bot effortlessly behind, which hovered a few inches above the ground.

"What do you think of Truxxe, Nathan?" asked Kayleesh.

"It's very… dark!" he exclaimed. "It's how Tom described it to me, I guess, but actually being here is so much more amazing. I mean, it's an alien planet — and we can breathe!"

"Yeah, it is pretty amazing," Tom grinned.

"Although a car would be nice. I'm getting a bit tired now."

"A what? Hey — see those green lights?" Kayleesh pointed a little way ahead of them. "That's our destination." Renewed by this news, the boys gathered speed, all eyes on the emerald hue.

A modest cluster of buildings made up the compound. Dwarfed by comparison to the titanic domain of TSS, the area comprises a central dome-roof structure surrounded by what looked like habitats. Green-tinged streetlamps lined neat little walkways between rows of apartment blocks and encircled the central building. There were a few dozen people milling about, chiefly Truxxian in species. There was no Wardrobian field in place here and so most people seemed to be dressed in local attire, not unlike the long employee robes Tom wore when on duty. It was refreshing to be somewhere not geared towards tourists - TSS, the Visitor's Centre. Perhaps this was the real Truxxe.

"This is Canmar Three," Kayleesh informed them. "A small town which pretty much keeps itself to itself. Not much employment here though, apart from the Job Selector. Ironic really! A lot of the inhabitants are either students or retirees. Canmar Three is home to one of Truxxe's three universities, which resides in the central building."

"Interesting stuff, Madame Tour Guide, but where do we need to go?" Nathan quipped.

"In there," Kayleesh pointed at the central edifice, which looked to Tom like a futuristic library from the outside. Traditional and earthly in style and yet it had an otherworldly impression about it. He wondered what material had been used to construct it — some kind of pure, metallic substance he couldn't quite identify. It was so difficult to make out much detail in this strangely lit town. It was all so dreamlike here.

Kayleesh switched off the ALSID bot to conserve power and secured it to a purpose-built post.

"How did you know about this place?" Tom asked Kayleesh.

"Oh, I like exploring — I found this town a long time ago. It's nice to get out of the service station for a while and absorb a little culture." Her violet eyes glinted a strange shade in the emerald glow of the street.

The Augtopian and the two Earthlings ascended a short flight of steps which led up to the entrance of the building: a gaping archway. The atmosphere inside was warm and lively without feeling overcrowded. A little way inside the spacious building Tom spotted a sign with the cumbersome wording; "Job Selector – Truxxian-Interplanetary Division," and made towards it. Tom was not sure what he was expecting - adverts on the wall, a computer terminal or a careers advisor. But he was taken aback when met with what looked like a row of holoceivers. They looked as though they were in the process of ingesting an entire class of students. He curiously observed the phenomenon from this new perspective as the Truxxians stepped inside the viscous bubble beings as he had done so before. He looked around at his friends. Was this the wrong place?

"I don't want to make a call," he protested. Kayleesh giggled.

"It's not a holoceiver exchange, Tom. They are holocreatures, certainly, but their psychic powers are put to a different use here." She ushered him towards one which was 'vacant'. "It looks like this one's free,"

"Hang on, why do I need to use one?" Tom pushed her away, scowling. He didn't trust them. After all, it was because one of these beings that Nathan had been abducted and arrested.

"It's only routine — it's to see what career you're suited too."

Nathan was gaping at the bobbing creatures which surrounded their customers with an expression of mixed amazement and disgust.

"But I am applying for a specific job for a specific reason. Serving burgers is not my ideal career path."

"I know, and they'll know that too once you step inside. Honestly, it's much quicker this way than all that form-filling!"

"If you say so," Tom shrugged with some reluctance and made his way over to the vacant, buoyant creature. He gulped then turned and whispered, "It won't know my reasons will it? I mean, why I want to get to Porriduum? I don't trust these-"

"These aren't as intelligent as the holoceiver beings," Kayleesh broke in. "Their minds are more singularly tracked -

nothing like the long-ranging communicators. They specialise in careers, relevant experience and location. Once they feed off the idea that your desire is to work on Porriduum, they'll bypass all potential motivation — Tom, *no one wants to work on Porriduum!*"

"Once again Kayleesh, you're not making me feel any better about things!" Tom shook his head and stepped inside the yellow holocreature.

Schlomm steered the "Prison Ship" Cluock towards the entrance of the mighty Porriduum. The real prison ships were flying in otherwise perfect tessellation with each other, seemed to be giving Schlomm's ship more than a wide birth — considerably more. He soon realised that the prisoner transporter ships were a good fifty times the size of his own small freight craft. The compositor meant that the other captains were perceiving his ship to be the size of their own when in fact, the Cluock was rattling around in its own pocket of space amongst these monstrosities.

At least there won't be any danger of crashing into anyone, he thought.

Schlomm checked his scanners. The flight window created by the solar eclipse was closing. Barely in the safety zone, the last of the prison ships followed the fleet into position, rendering the Glorbian trapped. There was no turning back now. Even if he could manage to weave his way back through the shoal of ships, and wasn't shot down, he was certain that the Gorgon's cruel eye would soon be peering round the planet once more and would irradiate anything in its view. Heart pounding, Schlomm grasped the controls tightly, as though he would otherwise fall out. Schlomm watched his monitor as one of the robust ships ahead of him slipped effortlessly through the molten crust of the planet to the access area like a penny dropping through rice pudding. Schlomm began to panic. Would the Cluock's resilience match that of a real Porriduum prison transporter ship? It may appear to be a prison ship on the outside, but the small freight craft was just a small freight craft. It wasn't designed to travel through the molten surface of a planet. The prison ships were rumoured to be made from the very elements found only on Porriduum. If this was true and only the hull of a Porriduum ship was likely to survive, then what was he doing here in a glorified burger van?

If Schlomm didn't think of a way out of this situation now, his ship was about to become part of the scalding rice pudding surface — with Schlomm a melted raisin within.

He couldn't go back, and he couldn't go forwards. Think, Schlomm. He began to panic and wished that Hannond were with him, although if he were, he wouldn't be in this situation to begin with. Oh, damn you, Hannond! Why did you get me into this? I'm about to be swallowed up by a planet!

What was that on the monitor? Was that an opening? It didn't look like a very large opening, but he was still some distance away from the craft in front of Schlomm Putt.

*I wonder if it's large enough for me to be able to dock inside that prison transporter ship. The Cluock will be safe within the hardy hull of one of those – and, more importantly, I'll be safe. I might be arrested on sight, but it's better than the alternative.*

Thinking quickly, the Cluock picked up speed as the Glorbian steered out of formation with the crawling fleet and made towards the aperture. He began to sweat, as it seemed that the crew had noticed their blunder as his point of access was beginning to close. With all of his concentration focussed on his diminishing goal, Schlomm didn't consider how this exploit looked from the exterior.

The compositor still operational, several hundred crew members in the vicinity watched their monitors in stunned incredulity as a ship as vast as the ones in which they were travelling seemed to have cut loose and was now heading for a collision with the ship in front of it. Just what was the foolish captain of that ship *doing?* Had he gone insane? Had he lost control – or worse, had one of the prisoners escaped their holding cell and hijacked the ship? The prospect of such a security breach sent a wave of panic throughout the flotilla.

It wasn't going to be the smoothest dock, Schlomm was certain of that. But if he didn't gather more speed, the ship he was aiming for would soon be engulfed by the prison planet before he could reach it. The Cluock would simply follow, burgers and all - into oblivion. He used all the skill he had gained in his experience as the Cluock Captain and aligned the ship with the now half-closed aperture, mere kilometres away. Stunned onlookers winced instinctively as the gargantuan craft headed for collision. The terrified captain in the ship behind the Cluock slammed on the retrograde rockets and prepared for impact.

# CHAPTER 11

"Please state desired occupation," the words resounded in Tom Bowler's head. What was his actual job title? How specific should he be? He didn't want to *cook* the food – he could barely make a toasted sandwich. Server? Attendant? Waiter? Restaurant cashier? Getting this wrong could be critical. These creatures are supposed to be telepathic, so surely they wouldn't quibble on semantics?

"I want to work on Porriduum – serving food," he said aloud.

A sudden humming noise resonated throughout the surrounding bubble. It was a strange, uncomfortable feeling, like being inside an organic refrigerator. Not that Tom had ever experienced that of course. What was it doing? Perhaps it was processing his request. Tom could see Nathan and Kayleesh through the yellow-tinged membrane of the bubble creature. He wished they didn't look so worried - it was most unnerving. They then seemed to be sharing a joke and Tom watched, as their shoulders shook with laughter -which was somehow worse. The humming ceased. Calm and androgynous, the voice echoed,

"You have the relevant experience." Tom smiled at the fact that the creature recognised this, although he thought that submitting an up-to-date curriculum vitae might be simpler. "Nevertheless, your IQ level suggests that you are over-qualified. Therefore, your application has been denied."

"What? But… but… I don't mind. I still want to work there!" Tom protested.

"Please select an alternative occupation or vacate," the composed voice stated.

"Wait, wait," there must be a way around this. "Er… let me… I want to work as a Porriduum guard!" he blurted in foolish desperation.

"Your IQ level suggest that you are over-qualified. Therefore, your application has been denied." it said again, the statement identical in tone as well as choice of phrase.

"OK, OK!" My IQ can't be that high if I can't think of a solution.

"Please select an alternative occupation or vacate."

"Well, what jobs on Porriduum are available which match my IQ?" Tom asked smugly and waited while the bubble rippled and hummed around him in deliberation. The humming ceased once more.

"There are presently zero opportunities available under the requested description. All higher skilled positions are currently filled."

"Thanks for nothing!" Tom yelled and made to thump his hand on the creature's skin in pure frustration. However, his hand passed through the membrane and the momentum of the action pulled him out of the creature, causing him to fall over. He stumbled to his feet. Undignified, he walked crossly over to his friends.

"Well?" Nathan asked, expectantly. "When do you start?"

"It's not that simple – my IQ is too high, apparently."

Nathan exploded into laughter. "You shouldn't be such a nerd, Tom."

"If you didn't have that tag around your wrist, I'd make you step inside that discriminating freak," Tom said, crossly.

"Stop it, you two," Kayleesh broke in. "We'll just have to think of something else."

"But we came all this way!" Tom exclaimed.

"Well, we'll have to make the most of our visit then," Nathan grinned. "I spy a Spotoon board."

Tom finished serving the last of the stragglers of another lunchtime rush and leant on the counter, chin cupped in his hands. It wasn't the same without Raphyl. He and Kayleesh hadn't noticed a huge increase in their workload since the apathetic Truxxian had been detained, but Tom missed his company. Mayty Reeston appeared from behind the shelving. He was gnawing a root vegetable of some kind with his large display of teeth.

"What's wrong, Tom? Upset you ran out of customers?" he asked cheerily. Tom sighed.

"I was just thinking about Raphyl. Do you think they're treating him badly in there?"

"On Porriduum? I'm not the one to ask – although I'm sure Jephle would have some answers for you."

"Jephle? Why, has he been there?" If Mayty had been born with eyebrows, Tom was sure that one of them would not only have raised but would be almost orbiting around his globular head. His expression suggested that Jephle had *definitely* been there and how hadn't Tom realised? Tom considered this notion. Jephle was the most dubious character Tom had encountered – save for the BBs. He always seemed to be acting surreptitiously, whether he was sitting in a team meeting or simply slicing fricumbers.

"Oh, yes," said Mayty. "It's probably why he keeps such a low profile." Mayty jabbed a thumb in the direction of the kitchen area.

"And what's your excuse?" laughed Tom. The bright-skinned being deposited the remainder of his snack into his mouth, most of it spurting out through his teeth as he said,

"Why don't you go and speak to him while it's quiet?"

Tom hesitated. He and Jephle were hardly the best of friends. It seemed to be rather a personal line of conversation to employ with someone he knew very little about. Mayty left Tom alone with his decision and went to speak with Kayleesh.

*Well, what have I got to lose?*

Tom found Jephle prowling around the kitchen area. When he noticed Tom's presence, he sheathed the kitchen knife he was holding into his robe pocket and he snapped around to face him. *Always so suspicious.*

"Hi Jephle," Tom said jovially.

"Tom," the small Truxxian replied quietly, grim faced.

"I was just thinking – it's strange here without Raphyl isn't it?" Tom said in what he hoped was a casual manner.

"Are you looking to replace your absent Truxxian friend with another?" Jephle said dryly, indicating that he meant himself. His expression didn't alter.

"Er…" Tom wasn't sure whether he was joking. Jephle's mouth cracked a smile - although it was not a pleasant one. Tom also noticed his hand creep to the pocketed knife. He smiled uneasily. "Well, I was just thinking that he's been on Porriduum for a few rotations now."

"Correct," Jephle blinked slowly.

"It must be very different being there -"

"If you wanted small talk, you should have chosen to have a conversation with a Strellion," he said curtly. "Now if you want to ask me about Porriduum, get to the point, boy!" Taken aback, Tom fumbled around for the right words.

"Er… OK… well… I was just wandering what it was like, really."

"It's a utopian dream world – beautiful gardens and nymph-like inhabitants."

"Really?"

"No, you brainless being - it's a prison planet!" The Truxxian snapped and shook his head. Tom noticed his grip tighten over the knife handle, his already pale knuckles whitening. He took a step back. The corner of Jephle's mouth curled upwards in a smile dripping with malice. What does he have against me? Mayty's never had trouble with him – as far as I know. Then his tone softened, in a manner which spiked icicles down Tom's back. "Tom, Porriduum is like…" he paused, swallowed. "Even the very memory of it chills me." Jephle's eyes glazed over, his mind evidently casting back to his time in Porriduum. His face twisted in recollection. "If Raphyl's in there, he won't be the same when he comes out." *Is that what happened to you?* Tom wanted to ask, but he decided to keep silent in an effort to keep clear of the proverbial eggshells.

"The pulsar star doesn't just stop people from escaping from Porriduum. Those infinitely powerful rays are also used *inside* the prison. Before I get to that I'll explain a bit more about the way in which the place is managed." Jephle paused, scratched his chin thoughtfully and continued.

"The prison needs to house the criminals from five thousand civilisations throughout two galaxies – Triangulum and Andromeda. Those civilisations are scattered across many different worlds with many different atmospheres. Of course, TSS get by this by mainly attracting clients who can comfortably walk around the station for a few hours or rotations. I'm sure you've seen non-oxygen breathing customers wearing tanks around the station? Well this is all very well for a short amount of time, but you can't have a prison full of long-term inmates who have to change their atmosphere cylinders every few hours. Therefore, there are many different sectors on the penal complex. Raphyl will be on one with an atmosphere very much like this one, his home planet. As was I."

"So, he'd be comfortable at least."

"If by comfortable you mean he'd be able to breathe, yes. No matter in which sector the prisoner is incarcerated, a universal security measure applies. You can't have cells partitioned off with bars – many aliens would be able to pass between them, whether they simply have lithe bodies, or the bars cannot hold their viscosity. But no creature from the far edge of the Triangulum galaxy to the distant reaches of Andromeda has a body which can survive Gorgon's deadly rays." Jephle shuddered at his own words.

"Picture an endless corridor stretching as far as the horizon – either side festooned with an infinite row of jail cells. Cell after cell after cell. Each accommodating two prisoners. Now, at first glance it would seem that each of these identical cells is missing a wall. It would appear that the inhabitants would be free to simply walk out of their cell at any time. However, if you looked closely you'd realise that in place of a solid wall – along the ceiling and along the floor are two pairs of vents, about so wide." The Truxxian indicated a small gap with his forefinger and thumb. "It's not a large gap, but it's large enough. One pair of vents comprises the main wall across the cell and remains on until a prisoner is transferred in or out of a cell."

"What are the vents for? Is it a force field?" Tom asked.

"Haven't you been listening to a word I have said?" Jephle scowled. "Force fields? No, the vents let Gorgon's rays through. Any prisoner who dares cross it will not live to do it a second time – I have seen it happen!"

"Oh!" Tom exclaimed, horrified. "But how does the light enter the prison? I thought that the entire complex existed beneath layers of molten rock?"

If you had ever seen a picture of Porriduum, you would have noticed that jutting out all over the planetoid are thousands of chimney-like structures, open to the sun, which reach deep down into the complex where the beam reaches the cells."

"OK." Tom's mind was whirring. "So, what happens when the planet is facing away from the neutron star? The entire surface doesn't face Gorgon's eye all the time! How do they get around that?"

"There's a series of prisms," Jephle said, simply. His expression remained harsh.

"Right. And these vents are used to control the inmates in every environment?"

"Clever isn't it?" Jephle's eyes glinted as he unsheathed his knife and stabbed an unsuspecting vegetable which had merely been minding its own business on the countertop. Tom took that as his cue to leave.

# CHAPTER 12

Tom Bowler stepped cautiously out of the lift and onto the complex's prison level. He felt uncomfortable enough about being in such close proximity to TSS's holding cells, let alone the idea of the harsh prison planet which held Raphyl. He was barely brave enough to come here alone. Suddenly, a pherobot clattered its way up to him and Tom appreciated its frustratingly pleasant affect. It emanated an ambiance of such beauty and wonder that at that moment Tom felt he would be unable to disobey any order that this creature asked of him. Should it open a cell door for example, Tom would have gladly stepped inside, with an inane smile on his face. Hey, he would have even swallowed the key himself. Fortunately, the robot did not abuse the powers it was programmed to possess and instead asked him in soft tones:

"Are you here to visit a prisoner?"

"Yes."

"Is the prisoner under maximum security or the tagging system?"

"Er… he has a tag," Tom answered truthfully. "I'm here to meet with Nathan Reed."

"Very well, please follow me," the robot turned, and Tom followed obediently, unable to prevent himself from looking at the pherobot's rather unusual, but nevertheless captivating behind as they walked. A double door hummed open for them at the detection of the robot guard's presence. They traversed through several octagonal blocks, each with three doors to both the left and the right, facing into the octagon. Tom was led through a door at one end of the block and out through another at the opposite end. Each block was identical in every way, save for the numbers coldly displayed in a surly, impersonal typeface on each cell door. Weaving and threading through the identical chambers in this honeycomb maze, the robot finally halted. It turned to Tom and slapped a green tag onto his right wrist. Tom gulped.

"Just a security measure," it purred. "I will remove it on your exit from the level." It then proceeded to open a cell door to the left of the chamber, which simply said "7A", and let Tom inside. Tom felt the pull of her pherobot field slowly ebb away as its clanging footsteps muted with distance.

"They do have a strange way of doing things here, don't they bud?" Nathan piped up as Tom entered his cell.

"Some things certainly take some getting used to." Tom agreed, tugging at his newly acquired green tag. "I thought you were allowed to wander the station?"

Nathan shrugged. "I am. But everything is monitored and double-checked and the time I am allowed out is restricted. It's not so bad though –"

"- Hey!" Tom interrupted. His head darted about the room, drinking in his surroundings. His mouth opened and closed several times, goldfish-like, in unreserved disbelief. "Your cell is not what I'd call a cell – in fact, it's better than my quarters! Much better!"

"What?" Nathan scratched his head.

"Just look at it – it's huge!"

Nathan shrugged, nonchalantly. He reclined into a plush, ergonomic chair and rested his hands on his stomach. Presently, he reached for a drink which had been resting on a nicely polished chrome table next to him, took a long sip through a zig-zag straw and belched. Tom continued to glare, incredulously. It was not only the space issue which both amazed and riled Tom, but the standard of the accommodation. It was a four-star hotel in comparison to his sparse apartment on level forty-two. Even the sparkly floor looked as though it had been swept by angels.

"It's not too bad is it?" said Nathan. "I think I'd be all right on Porriduum; you know."

Tom glared at his uninformed friend. "Nathan – from what I've heard today, this is a *palace* compared to Porriduum. No one has ever died from exposure to a pheromone field you know – well, not that I know of anyway," Tom began to tell Nathan exactly what Jephle had told him about the planet. Nathan sipped his drink and listened, transfixed. Tom paced up and down the cell like a caged lion, explaining and gesticulating as he told him about the horrors of Porriduum. "We have to get him out of there," he said finally.

"So, you keep saying, Tom, but look around you!" He waved his arms around the cell. "I think we're running out of options – you've tried to get a job there, you've researched the place, and you've still got one friend stuck in here. What do we do next?"

Before Tom could say that he really didn't know for the seventy-third time, he sensed the pherobot's presence and unthinkingly stood to attention.

"Just a security measure," the robot's sweet voice intoned from the other side of the cell door. "I will remove it on your exit from the level."

"Sorry I'm late," Kayleesh said as the metallic guard let her into the cell. Once the pherobot was out of earshot, she squealed, "Hyganty is going to lend us a Submian ship!"

"That's great!" Nathan enthused.

"But as we've said before we can't fly to Porriduum. We'd be fried. Besides, Nathan is tagged to Truxxe."

"The plan isn't to fly to Porriduum. Hyganty has been researching the prison itself…"

"… so have I," interrupted Tom, rather smugly.

"Really? Well then perhaps you'll also know that it was designed by ACD!" She blurted.

"Er…" Tom sat down on a lavish chair and gave Kayleesh one of his confused looks.

"Authority Construction Designs – you know, the company Raphyl's parents started? Their company designed Porriduum! It makes sense really as you can't get much more of an authoritative construction than a gigantic inter-galactic prison."

"So how does that information get us any closer to Raphyl?" Nathan asked.

"Well it's certainly useful to know and besides, it's not the only building they designed."

"The Parliamentary Building in the capital of Wheyland on Radiakka!" Nathan gushed. "If you fly out to Radiakka and take a look at that building, maybe it'll give you a better idea about Porriduum!"

"How did you know about that? Anyway, you're all insane!" exclaimed Tom. "Sorry," he remembered about Nathan's mother and realised what he had said when it as too late. Nathan shrugged, expressing his indifference. "But flying across the galaxy to have a look at some old building is not going to help free Raphyl."

"You're forgetting that we'll have Hyganty with us – he's born to investigate things like that."

"Oh I was forgetting about Sherlock Holmes," muttered Tom.

The Cluock rumbled to a stop. It wasn't the smoothest of landings and the ship was hissing and whining in places it shouldn't, but its captain was alive. He shut off the engine and the compositor too to save power and glared at the monitor. He had docked into the underbelly of the ship and was relieved to find that he was not in the prisoner hold. But where had he docked? And how would he get out of here? Schlomm's plan had not extended any further than simply staying alive.

A figure passed soundlessly across the screen. It was stunted in height, and corpulent. What was that? A guard, perhaps? Schlomm's sense of sneakiness returned, as did his wide grin. He kept his eyes on the monitor. There it was again – it appeared to be alone. He activated the ship's scanners. His suspicions were confirmed – only one life-form within the immediate locality.

Slowly, slowly, catchy Malform, thought the Glorbian. Schlomm's devious mind had conjured up a new plan. If he could get a closer look at the guard, he would be able to see whether his uniform would be suitable for Schlomm to use as a disguise. The fleeting shape of the figure had hinted at the possibility. Now, how to get a closer look without being questioned, arrested or worse? If only he had a weapon. The *ship* had a weapon, he realised. It wasn't equipped with a deadly armoury, it being a meat delivery vehicle, but there was always the orange lever. Schlomm had pulled it once before to render unconscious a herd of stampeding hoofabeasts on the planet Smechana IV. The comtosa gas it released had temporarily knocked them out, thus allowing him to deliver the consignment without being pulverised into Schlomm jam. He suspected that using the same amount of gas in such a confined space would have a bigger effect on the lone guard. Schlomm didn't necessarily want to have the guard's blood on his hands, if he could help it, so he pulled the lever just a little way along its furrow.

After a few moments, a cloud of pink, unfurling smoke began to wisp out of the vents which were stationed all around the perimeter of the ship. Soon, the gas particles had congregated into a soft haze. Happenstance had it that Schlomm's target was just in view on the ship's monitor. The Glorbian observed a kaleidoscope of expressions on the guard's face; confusion, horror, panic, then came a soft thud as the small body hit the floor. Schlomm grinned a toothy grin and waited for the gas to settle.

Shielding his mouth and nose by pressing a piece of old rag Schlomm had found on the bridge onto his mouth, he alighted from the ship. The air stung his eyes slightly, but he was still alert and awake. He padded over to the fallen guard and proceeded to strip him of his uniform with his one free hand, which was quite a challenge. He pulled the taupe-coloured, slightly snug-fitting shirt over his plump body and pulled the lower garments up to his waist, if you could call it that. The legs were trailing on the floor a little but otherwise, it wasn't an entirely odd fit. Lastly, he crammed his feet into the guard's shoes and gave a satisfied grunt. He glanced at the now naked guard, who had made the unfortunate decision that day to not wear any underwear. Schlomm shook his head and dropped the old rag over the man's private area which only served to make the unconscious watchman look all the more pathetic.

# CHAPTER 13

The towering Submian strutted along the line of companions like a sergeant inspecting his squad. He held in his pincers, a trio of visitor passes to the Wheyland Parliamentary Building, which he distributed as though he were awarding medals for bravery. His multi-faceted insectile eyes blinked. His expressionless face somehow bared an aura of conceit. Kayleesh, Frarkk, and finally Tom were presented with the passes, which Hyganty pinned onto their compsuits.

"We now all have the right to enter the Wheyland Parliamentary Building on Radiakka," the praying-mantis form announced. "At least – we have access to some of the areas."

"Well done, Hyganty," Kayleesh beamed.

*Well done? Does simply contacting a Radiakkan tourist board to request tour passes warrant praise?* Tom felt his envy rise – he was as green as the Submian he resented. Tom wished that Nathan were with their party – he longed to show him that the universe had more to offer than the planet Truxxe. He was excited about the fact that he was going to take a trip to yet another planet. Radiakka sounded more hospitable than the other planets he had visited since leaving the Earth. He yearned for the warmth of sunshine on his back, which Truxxe unquestionably lacked. He wondered what excitement Wheyland had to offer and hoped that they would come closer to finding a way to help Raphyl. If only Raphyl were able to contact them again – then Tom could ask him about his friend's parents and what really happened all those years ago.

The four voyagers embarked on the Submian ship, to which Tom was no stranger. Tom and Kayleesh went directly to their flight chairs and Hyganty and Frarkk made their way to the bridge to join the rest of the crew. Tom grew slightly anxious as he strapped himself into the chair, recalling the horrifying feeling of previous launches aboard the ship. He didn't think he'd ever get used to the feeling of his eyeballs being sucked towards his toes.

"Are you all right, Tom?" Kayleesh asked, settling into her seat.

"Me? Yes, I'm fine," Tom lied. Why couldn't he be as calm as Kayleesh?

"I know it's not a pleasant take off, but we'll soon be there," she smiled. Her warm words comforted him.

It was a relatively short journey, but Tom was still glad to land. The travellers stepped out into the brightness of the Wheyland port. Tom wished that his compsuit could compensate for the difference in temperature because he felt as though he was wearing a wetsuit in the desert. He realised with horror that he'd forgotten to apply deodorant that morning and gave his right armpit a sly sniff. He grimaced.

Wheyland's port was of a modest size in comparison to Truxxe's – the far walls occupied the same time zone for one thing. But the one thing Radiakka did have in common with Truxxe was the amount of tourism is attracted. Tom watched with amusement as a crowd of excited passengers boarded an open-top shuttle bus which had brightly painted livery. The holidaymakers fought their way to the top deck for the seats with the best view. They still hadn't settled down when the bus produced a resounding PARP! and without warning it started up suddenly, causing half of the passengers to fall into the laps of the other half. Tom chortled out loud at the absurdity and no sooner had the bus disappeared out of sight that an identical one pulled up in its place.

"How far is it to the Parliamentary Building, Hyganty?" asked Kayleesh.

"Too far to walk, I'm afraid. But our passes include transport."

"Nice!" smiled Kayleesh.

Hyganty and Frarkk strode ahead – in the direction of the shuttle bus.

"We're not going in that," Tom protested.

"What's wrong with it?" Kayleesh demanded. "It moves doesn't it?"

"It's just that... well... we'll look like such tourists."

"Well, we *are!* And since when did that matter to you?"

Tom sighed and followed the others onto the bus. He showed his pass to the driver and made his way up the steps with the other passengers, but not without first being elbowed in the ribs by a spiky appendage which didn't exactly resemble an elbow. He also suffered a mouthful of hair from a large shaggy creature who obviously hadn't even heard of shampoo. Just when Tom thought that he was going to fall back down the steps with nothing but another spiky creature to break his fall, an arm grabbed his own and jerked him forwards.

"I've found us some seats." It was Kayleesh. Tom squeezed his way past a group of Truxxians and spotted the vacant seat ahead of him.

The bus then chose that moment to emit its loud PARP! and Tom knew that he had very little time to take his seat. When the bus didn't start immediately, however, Tom relaxed a little. Maybe this one has a more considerate driver. But his confidence was crushed when a second later he found himself face-first into the lap of the hairy beast who's fur he'd already sampled quite enough of that day. Apologising to the creature and avoiding eye contact with a hysterical Kayleesh, Tom finally took his place next to Frarkk.

The crowded vehicle left the spaceport and journeyed into the wide streets of Wheyland. The passengers looked about them, drinking in the grand buildings around them and the cloudless sky above.

"Welcome to Tops Tours!" A wiry automaton with a megaphone for a mouthpiece rose out of the metal deck at the front of the bus. Tom deduced that there must have been an ALSID unit on board. The ALSID had chosen to translate the android's voice to have an irritating, brash tone to authenticate the vehicle's over-confident tour guide. "On your right you will notice the spectacular Basilica of Nampoony, built nine generations ago by the early Wheylanders. The building took just four hundred rotations to make, which is incredible considering they didn't have the technology which we have today," the desperately perky robot said in its cheery manner.

"And coming up on our left is the astounding Office of Victory, home to the Chief Minister herself." Tom's ears twitched. The Chief Minister? This surely meant that the Parliamentary Building could not be far away.

"The Chief Minister is away in the southern hemisphere this rotation, so it is unlikely that we will chance upon her." Some groans of disappointment rippled through the rows of sightseers. "Although some party members may be around the Parliamentary Building itself. Now, the award-winning Parliamentary Building was built more recently, just four generations ago, planned and designed by the renowned ACD." Tom's ears pricked up and he was sure that he spotted Kayleesh's waggle. The bus meandered around a bend and a glorious structure filled the horizon, accompanied by gasps of awe. The guide continued. "Notice the sweeping rooftops and the soaring towers, beautiful yet robust in its design. The enchantment and splendour of a fairy-tale castle, spliced with the fortitude and security of a citadel. Security is paramount in this building," warned the automaton, his words modified to more serious tones. "So be sure to retain your passes at all times. All visitors have amber passes which means that you are able to follow the routes within the amber-marked areas only. Those who stray off the allotted routes will have to accept the penalty of their actions." There was an unnerving pause while the megaphone mouthpiece moved slowly from left to right as though surveying its audience. Whether or not the robot was blind – Tom could not spot a pherobot-esque camera on this peculiar façade – he still felt as though they were being scrutinised. The robot then regained its composure, a jovial guide once more, and continued in its previous manner. "The Parliamentary Building contains two thousand rooms…" that's almost double that of the Houses of Parliament, Tom recalled from a year nine school trip to London, "…five miles of corridors and contains ceremonial suites, offices, dining rooms, galleries, lobbies and libraries. Additionally, there is a whole range of functional suites, the purpose of which I am not programmed to reveal." Tom and Kayleesh glanced at each other.

"We shall soon be arriving at the first stop. If you wish to continue to the next point of interest, the Baths of Grungha, please remain seated." The bot folded itself up like an inelegant music stand and disappeared back into floor.

They rose to leave. Fortunately, only a third of the passengers stood up, so the stampede of disembarking passengers was less traumatic than when they had boarded the bus. However, a smaller tourist group would mean that it would be more difficult for the four of them to drift away from the crowd unnoticed once inside the building. Moreover, how were they going to wander off the amber zones without suffering the consequences?

# CHAPTER 14

Tom toyed with the visitor pass which was attached to his compsuit. It glistened green through to amber, as he twisted it gently in the bright sunlight. In a small typeface the words spread across it in two rows; "Wheyland Parliamentary Building visitor. Standard pass."

PARP! The bus pulled away behind them.

"Are we all convened?" Another robotic guide unexpectedly appeared out of a metallic booth on the side of the road. Its voice was identical to that of the bus guide although this one was equipped for walking. It was much more robust-looking, strong legged. Its arms flailed about as it spoke, perhaps to appear more enthusiastic about its duty. In one of its metallic hands, the guide was clutching a green flag which it waved, beacon-like, above its head. "Welcome to The Wheyland Parliamentary Building. I assure you all that you will have a pleasurable and safe visit with us today. You are free to wander around each room as we pass through, but should you lose me I am the one waving the green flag!"

*You're also the seven-foot high robot!* Tom sniggered to himself.

"I will be giving you a brief description of the history and function of each room," he continued. "Although should you require in-depth information – I know that many of you are students who may need a more detailed experience – there are information points along the way. The ALSID system ensures that these are accessible for all patrons."

"I think we'll need more than the student experience," Kayleesh whispered to Tom. He nodded, still laughing at the flag-waving bot at the front of the group.

"Additionally, there will be a young man on his work experience placement accompanying us on the tour today so feel free to ask him anything regarding the tour and he will endeavour to use the knowledge he has gained so far to help you."

"Hyganty," Kayleesh whispered to the Submian. "How are you planning to escape the group?"

He merely waved a dismissive claw. "Patience, Kayleesh."

Tom didn't see why they had to be so secretive about it. Kayleesh looked as frustrated about the situation as he felt.

A heavy-looking door sealed the entrance to the citadel. The robot stood in front of a panel on the stone wall beside it while the expectant group looked on. The panel flashed, having apparently made a link with something on the robot's torso.

"Please step back," advised the guide. It was good advice to heed by, for a moment later the door began to grind outwards; the thickest door that Tom had ever seen. If this was where the ministers were stationed, he wondered how thick the door to Porriduum was. And still it continued to grind open. Just as Tom was beginning to think that the door was in fact a cube, the entrance was finally visible. It ground slowly to a halt.

"Welcome!" The guide reiterated. The tourists filed through. Some trod cautiously, while others were eager and brazen, jostling their way to the front. Tom and his companions made their best efforts to linger at the back. Once inside, they were greeted by a small humanoid being, his skin was dark purple in colour and his straight teeth shone brightly. He radiated youth and enthusiasm and Tom surmised that he was the fellow on his work placement. No non-robotic long-term employee gave this air of goodwill and zeal. Except, perhaps, Kayleesh.

Tom gaped open-mouthed at lofty crystalline walls, festooned with portraits of what he presupposed to be celebrated luminaries of past and present. The portraits hung fifteen, twenty feet tall, looming over the group as they passed through. The style of the paintings was alien in every respect; a style which Tom couldn't place in regard to anything from Earth's art history. He couldn't even imagine what implements were used to create the works as they seemed to shimmer in and out of reality. Quite unlike the garish holograms of the advertisements he had been bombarded with at the service station, these pictures seemed to display more than colour and light. They appeared to go within themselves somehow and they also gave the impression that they could look into the soul of the onlooker. Not in the way that an art historian may describe the eyes of the Mona Lisa to be following the viewer around the room, but in an almost literal sense, Tom felt almost invaded by the glares of the faces. Feeling both uncomfortable and awe filled by these images, Tom found it a challenge to take his eyes off them. Even the guide's sudden brash, buoyant tones couldn't break his trance.

"Many of the early paintings in this hall are from the Rahngram era, when experiments with the spectrum of the rare and costly yieldstone were predominant amongst the gentry. You will notice how the artists have captivated the character of the subject of each portrait which subsequently radiates from the canvas, luring in the viewer. It is well known that the combined energy from this collection delivers an incredible effect, I am sure that you will all agree," said the robot, whose metallic brain was perceptibly oblivious to the effects which he was trying to describe.

"The marble floor was imported…"

But Tom didn't care about the origin of the marble floor. He couldn't stop thinking that the fifth generation Chief Minister was looking into his very being and trying to discover what he was up to. Tom's eyes narrowed, focussing on the glare of the aged being in the painting. The portrait didn't move exactly, but it seemed to swoop from one plane to another, taking Tom with it. He heard a voice; an echo.

"Tom!" Kayleesh's warm hands cupped his face. He blinked and looked at her, startled. "Are you all right?"

"Yes," Tom raised an uncertain eyebrow. Then he said quickly, "I think we should go our own way as soon as we can – I'm not sure I like it in here." Kayleesh nodded and swallowed hard.

"I know what you mean."

Tom noticed that the two Submians seemed to be speaking clandestinely amongst themselves.

"I wonder what they're planning." Tom whispered.

"I don't know, but I'm sure they know what they're doing," shrugged Kayleesh. A look of horror suddenly came over her face. "Tom – what's happened to him?" The young man who was on work experience seemed to be having some kind of seizure.

Schlomm made to exit the hold but halted when he heard faint voices outside the door. He pressed his ear against the cold metal.

"Sentry One Nine Three, what took you so long?" A strong, authoritative voice barked.

"Apologies – Sentry One Nine Three reporting for duty," came the nervous reply, followed by the crisp stamp of a foot.

"Right, well I trust that hold seven is secure?"

"Er… certainly sir."

"Hmm you don't *sound* very certain, One Nine Three. Fortunately for you I don't have time to check the vigilance of every single guard," growled the first voice. "The prisoners in Bay Eleven are about to disembark. We need as many staff members as we have convicts for that shipment, so off you go. And by the way," there was a pause and then Schlomm heard him tell Sentry One Nine Three, menacingly, "they're class one prisoners!"

Schlomm literally heard the second speaker gulp in terror. *What were class one prisoners?* He wondered. *Kidnappers? Murderers? Torturers?* A moment later, he heard the decrescendo of rapid footsteps on a metallic floor. The owner of the commanding voice uttered a few incoherencies and then more footsteps - this time disappearing in the opposite direction - confident, striding.

Schlomm knew that he couldn't hide in the hold forever. He had to act the part; act confidently. He didn't want to be perceived as pathetic and weak like Sentry One Nine Three. According to the name tag on the uniform he had stolen, he was Sentry One Four One. He wondered whether the number had any significance of rank. He wondered what number the other voice had – One Four Zero? Ten? One, perhaps?

Schlomm needed to know the most probable place that Hannond would be incarcerated. One small Hannond on an entire planet. Why had he even attempted this exploit? He wondered whether he was the only inter-galactic criminal ever to have broken *into* Porriduum. Schlomm pulled himself up as tall as he could, gave a sharp exhale of breath and told himself; *You are Sentry One Four One, you are Sentry One Four One.* He adopted his gruffest expression, opened the heavyweight door and marched resolutely along the curved passageway. Grey, oppressive walls surrounded him, the occasional heavy-duty door to the left and right, the sound of his booted feet on metallic floor. Momentarily, he could hear several pairs of booted feet approaching ahead of him. Mustering up his courage and preparing himself for confrontation, Schlomm continued his steady progression in the direction of the advancing footsteps.

He was surprised to encounter, not a group of sentries or prisoners he had expected, but a single guard. The guard, Sentry One Six Three as advertised on his uniform, had an elongated body which snaked far back along the passageway. Many booted feet met the ground, caterpillar-like, poking out of the bottom of the dozen trouser legs of his uniform. Schlomm was glad that he hadn't had to borrow *this* creature's uniform - getting the thing off his immobile body would have been trial enough. And he was no seamstress.

"Sentry One Six Three?" Schlomm addressed the beast, bravely, using his most authoritative tone. He had spoken before he could even realise the stupidity of his own actions. To his surprise, One Six Three stopped abruptly and faced him.

"Sentry One Six Three reporting for duty!" All of his right feet stamped in unison, obediently, resulting in an almighty thunderclap.

"I have a little security test for you." Schlomm hoped that his hastily constructed plan would work. *Please let the numbers have significance of rank!* The prospect of twelve kicks in the teeth wasn't a pleasant one. "One Six Three, how would one go about getting to the section containing… er… perpetrators of hate crime? The type who would, for instance, burn another nation's flag?"

"Which specific environment?" he responded, the voice more self-assured than that of Sentry One Nine Three.

"Er…" *Don't let your uncertainty give you away!* Schlomm cursed himself. He thought quickly. "An air breather – the same as the air in this passageway; a ground-dweller."

"The section containing seventy-eight percent nitrogen, twenty-one percent oxygen and one percent carbon dioxide harbouring Class Four prisoners who can endure in this specific atmosphere is Sector Two," the amply-limbed sentry replied, smugly. He had the air of a Straight-A student awaiting the proverbial pat on the back. Schlomm despised self-satisfied clever clogs, especially ones with more clogs than most. However, he was delighted to have received such a detailed reply. He continued to play along; school master to the pupil.

"Very good, One Six Three. And how would one get to Sector Two?" The knowledgeable creature narrowed his eyes, distrustfully. Had Schlomm gone too far? Why hadn't he quit while he was ahead? He felt sweat on his brow but tried to remain his composure.

"By using the assigned digi-maps of course," Sentry One Six Three replied.

"Very good One Six Three," Schlomm said through gritted teeth. And added, daringly, "I trust that you're on your way to Bay Eleven to escort the Class One convicts?"

"Yes, sir," he nodded his huge caterpillar head and continued along the corridor. *Too smart for his own good,* Schlomm thought as the creature's behind finally passed him as he clomped his way up the passageway. *Although only in a bookish way, retaining numbers and the like. Had he been that smart he wouldn't have given me all that information so willingly. Perhaps the rumours were true, on balance. Now how do I get hold of a digi-map?*

# CHAPTER 15

Tom gaped at the poor temporary worker who was mid-seizure; writhing and convulsing on the stone floor. The attention of the entire crowd was soon upon him.

"Will everyone please stand back while I engage First Aid mode?" the guide requested, making its way through the crowd.

"There is no need, I am more than qualified! I have seen this reaction before," piped up a confident voice. It was Frarkk. The Submian elbowed his way through to the patient. Kayleesh and Tom looked at one another and mouthed in perfect synchronisation;

"Frarkk is a doctor?"

The two of them tried to get a closer look, to infiltrate the cluster of congregating bystanders, but the heaving mass would not dispel.

"Please give the doctor a little more room to work," the guide demanded. The group retreated a little, but not enough for Tom and Kayleesh to be able to see just what Frarkk was doing. Above the ruckus the guide spoke again: "The doctor has requested the assistance of a Tom Bowler." Tom froze. He didn't know anything about medicine. What could he do? "Tom Bowler," the guide repeated.

Tom looked at Kayleesh, who simply shrugged. He took a step forwards and the multi-coloured sea of creatures parted, creating a path. On the floor in front of him, Frarkk was knelt over the convulsing body of the patient. He gestured for Tom to join him so Tom obeyed and knelt next to the praying mantis creature. He looked at the pallid figure on the floor. Before he could speak, the Submian leant close and whispered in his ear. At the same time, he felt a pincer on his chest and his top pocket became heavy.

"Take this pass and get to the restricted areas," he whispered. "Don't ask questions. This could be our only chance."

"How did you – did you do this to him?" Tom asked in terror, "You did something to him on purpose so you could steal-"

"Shh," Frarkk warned and then said aloud, role playing for the purpose of the audience, "Tom please could you reassure the patient while I administer the solution?" Tom played along and took the patient's left hand and spoke to him in soft tones, although he wasn't sure whether he was even conscious. Frarkk reached into his compsuit pocket and revealed a small electronic device. He pressed the device to the inside of the fitting man's cheek and within seconds his movements ceased. His chest began to rise and fall peacefully; his face slowly relaxed; his teeth unclenched; purple returned to the cheeks; a smile emerged.

"Seizure triggered by the yieldstone spectrum," Frarkk said by way of explanation. He plopped the device back into his pocket and helped the man stand up. "It's not uncommon."

"Sir I would like to know where you got that device. Are you a real doctor?" the guide asked, seemingly unused to be the one asking the questions. Frarkk, however, ignored the query and said, curtly,

"You'll be lucky if this chap doesn't sue – I don't remember seeing a warning sign on entry to the building." The guide, retreating from the group was then bombarded by a flurry of protestations and questions from the crowd. "Here's your chance!" Frarkk whispered to Tom, amid the mounting brouhaha. "GO!"

Tom slipped away from the commotion to where Kayleesh was waiting. He took the pass out of his pocket and waved it at her. It was shimmering green through amber to a sumptuous ruby red.

*Wheyland Parliamentary Building employee. Premium pass,* the pass proudly stated across its width. Kayleesh beamed at him and ushered for him to go. After all, there was only one pass.

But where to go? He glanced at the mass of tourists. They would only be distracted momentarily. He looked about him. There were five other doors leading off the grand hallway. Two of them had a red glow about them and he presumed that these came under the red zone, thus requiring a premium pass. Quickly, Tom approached one of these premium pass doors and showed his badge to the panel. He was relieved when the door hushed silently open. There was no one on the other side of the door. Tom paused and took a moment to absorb the situation.

Had Frarkk and Hyganty *planned* what he witnessed happen to the work experience boy? Had they caused it? And if so, how? Was it actually anything to do with the yieldstone spectrum? Or was it something to do with the strange device in Frarkk's pocket? Also, had he known that the effect wasn't fatal and that he would recover, or was it pure chance? But the question which perplexed Tom the most was, had the plan always been to send Tom out on his own; the only one who had acquired a premium pass? Were the other three just part of the decoy or did they each have another part to play in all of this? Was Kayleesh any wiser than he? Tom wished that the secret party he had become involved with didn't act so secretly.

*I suppose it's down to me then,* Tom shrugged. *But what am I even meant to be looking for?*

The corridor in which Tom now found himself was speckled with crimson footlights. It seemed that they liked to make the point that this was a red zone. Tom checked that his badge hadn't spontaneously turned into a chicken or - even worse - a standard pass, and made his way gingerly along the corridor. He wondered whether Porriduum had different zones according to hierarchy. Were some prisoners allowed more privileges than others? Were some staff members granted access to areas that others were not authorised to be admitted? He suspected that the answer to both of these questions was yes but doubted that the system here would bear any similarity to that on the prison planet. The coloured zones would not necessarily be the brainchild of the architects; it was unlikely that Raphyl's parents would have devised the security system for either structure. But then what did the buildings have in common if any? What kind of clues was he expected to find here? He wished that Kayleesh were with him.

Suddenly a door to his left opened and a peculiar looking, but strangely attractive, alien emerged. She was almost humanoid, save for two pairs of gills on either side of her mouth. They opened and closed rhythmically. She smiled at him.

"Hello, are you new?" Her voice was surprisingly deep and rich. Her shoulder-length, burnt-orange coloured hair framed her round face. Her features were more pronounced than those of the delicate Kayleesh and she had a markedly stockier build. She was a good seven feet tall and had the demeanour of a top athlete. She looked as though she could pick Tom up with one hand and throw him across the corridor, but her eyes implied that she wouldn't. The girl wore a green jersey which served to emphasise her emerald eyes. The jersey bore a badge identical to Tom's ill-gotten one.

"Hello. Yes, I think I got a bit lost," lied Tom.

"Where are you going? I'm going to the canteen across the way if that's what you're looking for."

"Yes, I was looking for the canteen," he lied again. "I'm Tom Bowler," he added,

"Gracer Menille," the girl smiled, her gills habitually opening and closing. She strode over to the opposite side of the passageway and the door opened to reveal a spacious cafeteria. The abundantly decorated high ceiling gave even a simple workers' eatery a sense of grandeur. Crescent-shaped recesses lay in the room's four, slightly concave, walls. Each recess harboured a globular light fitting, emitting a soft yellow glow. The serenely decorated space was in contrast to the lively assemblage of workers which inhabited it. Arms, tentacles and trays jostled about the lunch queue and Tom was quickly reminded of his job at the express cuisine restaurant.

As they approached the long food counter, Gracer warned him.

"Don't expect too much – I think they offer more variety in prison!" "Prison? Which prison?" Tom asked, taken aback, but his words were lost as his lunch companion was already reeling off her order to the attendant in her vociferous tones.

"I'll have my usual fried volubabeast steak with one of each vegetable and a side order of skewered kweets. Oh, and I'd better have a mug of julmie juice to go with it, please."

Tom encountered the same problem he had when he had first arrived on Truxxe; he was overwhelmed by a completely unrecognisable menu. Over the past few months, he had become accustomed to some of the foods available at the service station - although he wasn't sure that his digestive system had. He faltered a while and finally plumped for a burger in a bun and a ruffleberry milkshake which seemed to be the safest option. It was fortunate that the canteen accepted Ds as payment, although the cashier did raise two of her eyebrows. It was even more fortunate that Gracer did not notice that he was paying with Truxxian currency. He did not want to appear like a tourist.

"Is that all you're having?" Gracer asked. Tom shrugged and took a small bite out of his burger. Gracer didn't seem to eat, as much as refuel. The speed at which food was transferred from plate to gullet was astonishing. There seemed to be a constant stream of meat and vegetables being consumed and Gracer didn't stop for breath, although her gills were opening wider and at shorter intervals, as though to compensate. Far from being repelled, however, Tom was spellbound. He slowly chewed on his first mouthful as he watched this beast of a girl devour her feast. By the time Tom was half-way through his burger, Gracer had finished her meal and was making light of her julmie juice which wasn't so much of a mug as a decanter. Tom sipped his milkshake, his eyes still on her. Gracer set down the now empty mug and remarked in quite serious tones,

"You humanoids have strange eating habits!" Her dark, curious, dark eyes studied his face.

Tom couldn't prevent himself from laughing. Once he had calmed down he decided to get back to the plan. He needed information.

"So, Gracer, how long have you worked here?"

"Me? About 15 cycles of this planet – half my life, in fact!" Her answer did not tell Tom anything. How old was she? The same age as Kayleesh? No, maybe a little older.

"Is this your first day, then?" she asked him.

"Yes I'm er... I'm on work experience." Tom tried to steer the conversation away from himself. "Do you know much about this building? It's just that it's so intricate and interesting. I was wondering whether there was anything like trap doors, secret passageways...?"

Gracer laughed, "What a funny fellow you are! Trap doors? Secret passageways? Not some kind of spy, are you?"

Tom almost splatter painted Gracer's green jersey in ruffleberry milkshake, in surprise. "No, no of course not. I just enjoy... exploring. I'm fascinated by unusual structures and architecture." Tom hoped that his further lies wouldn't lead to questioning. What if Gracer was an enthusiast and asked him which architects he liked? Other than Raphyl's parents, could he name even *one?* But Gracer's mind didn't work in the same way as most people's.

"It's a shame you're not a spy," she remarked, curiously. "That would be fun. But then again... if you *were* one you wouldn't have come right out and questioned an employee about secret passageways," she guffawed. Tom saw a glimmer of childlike innocence in her eyes.

"True," Tom laughed along.

"Which is a shame, because being in cahoots with a spy would break up an otherwise dull existence," she said playfully.

Tom leaned in close and whispered, "Well, we could pretend we were spies. You and me, we could play at being undercover agents."

"That sounds a lot more interesting than architecture!"

"Indeed. So, where do we start?"

# CHAPTER 16

The familiar smell of grilled meat led Sentry One Four One further along the corridor to the staff canteen. His stomach was so hollow now that it was as though it had unconsciously escorted him there. He began to salivate. Schlomm's shrewd trait caused him to wonder for a moment where Porriduum sourced its meat. If he could supply the prison with a regular shipment, he and Hannond would be fantastically wealthy from a sole client. He filed the thought under *New Business Ideas* in his astute mind and switched his thoughts back to his vacant belly, which was plying for attention.

The high walls and beautifully decorated ceiling of the canteen were in sharp contrast to the monotonous corridor outside. Twelve crescent-shaped recesses lined the walls - each one occupied by a spherical light.

A thirteenth spherical object hung in the air, alone and rebellious, almost brushing the ceiling. It bobbed about, completely disregarded by all.

Schlomm was too focussed on food to notice his surroundings, as his flat feet padded their way to the serving counter. Before he could feast his beady eyes on the choice of cuisine, however, Schlomm realised with horror that he wasn't carrying any money. He felt inside the pockets of his stolen uniform in desperation and uncovered three objects. He held out the contents in a fat, greasy fist to the Augtopian attendant, a tarnished metal disc, a wooden peg and a sticky rubber bung. The attendant glared at the articles for a few moments and brushed his long, golden hair behind his shoulder and sighed. He peeled the bung from the Glorbian's clammy grasp and examined it.

"Haven't you got anything smaller?" the attendant mumbled.

"Well, how much will this buy me?" Schlomm licked his lips expectantly.

"Sir, you could buy the entire canteen with this piece," he sighed again.

Schlomm considered the offer for a moment. He *was* hungry. The growing queue behind him was becoming audibly impatient - one or two of them were banging their canteen trays on the counter. Being the sole cause for a hungry, irate workforce would not be the best way for Schlomm to integrate himself. As much as he wanted to take all the food for himself and tell the queue where they could shove their empty trays, he remained calm for the sake of the mission. He had to remain inconspicuous.

The attendant was running his delicate fingers through the contents of the till. He shrugged.

"Let me see… if you buy a *splendid sized ravenous meal*, I can give you five hundred shards change. I think that's the best I can do."

Schlomm agreed and was soon heaving a heavy-laden tray to the nearest vacant table. The attendant had provided him with two bags full of change in the form of jingling plastic, which he had pegged to either side of Schlomm's uniform as though he were a Urgarzian packhorse. The bulging, clinking bags were doing little to help Schlomm's attempted surreptitious movement. Schlomm growled into his splendid sized burger. Now he'd have to get rid of five hundred shards of their ridiculous currency. Of course, he could just *dump* the coins somewhere. He could give them away or hide them. But this was Schlomm Putt and Schlomm Putt did not willingly abandon money. It was not his way. He would have to find some way of investing it. He chewed slowly, his taste buds barely registering the flavour, as the cogs in his mind began to clank round.

Sentry Nine and sentry One One One sat down at Schlomm's table. The complexion of both humanoid beings was pallid, as though their skin hadn't seen any sunlight for weeks - which was quite likely. One of them possessed a shifty grin and was toying with his food. The other ate ravenously, brown sauce raining onto his tray. Schlomm would rather have been left to think in peace but was soon glad that they had chosen his table.

Nine whispered something incoherent to his slovenly companion.

"Eh uh urr-eeen!" the sloppy eater mumbled in reply through an extra-large mouthful of food.

Nine looked at him in disgust.

"I didn't catch any of that!" Can you say it again after you've swallowed that sandwich?"

One One One sighed, spraying vegetable particles across the table as he did so. He chewed quickly and tried again.

"Well if you will ask when I've got a mouthful of food – I said *sector thirteen!*"

His companion's eyes widened.

"Keep your voice down!"

"Sorry, I thought you wanted me to say it clearly."

"Yes, but I didn't want you to broadcast it!"

One One One shrugged and took an even larger bite, perhaps to spite him.

"I hope you don't think I'm being nosey – but what exactly is happening in sector thirteen?" enquired Schlomm.

"Now see what you've done?" Nine scowled at the slovenly guard.

Schlomm shifted in his seat. As he did so the coin bags announced their presence, jangling at his side. Nine's ears pricked up. His scowl turned to a smile. "Sounds like you have money to cook, Sentry One Four One. In that case you may well be interested in sector thirteen!"

"What is sector thirteen?"

"Hmm I'm not sure if I should tell you – you're above a One Three Zero."

"Stop playing games!" Schlomm growled.

"Games are exactly what you will be playing if you go there," he smiled. "Sector thirteen is where the gambling room is."

Tom tried to stop staring at Gracer Menille's gills. Look at her eyes Tom, she has lovely eyes. But her eyes were facing forwards and her gills were puffing in and out mere inches from his face as they walked the corridors of the Wheyland Parliamentary Building. It was hard *not* to look at them. Gracer was giving him a tour. In effect they were "playing" as spies. She was a ten-year-old in the body of a basketball player. He humoured her as she was undoubtedly humouring him.

"So, where to?"

"Tom! You have to stay in character! We're not explorers – we need to be on some kind of mission. Hmm… I know. We could find out about Radiakka II!"

"Radiakka II?"

"Yes – the proposed second planet. Surely you've heard of it?"

"No, I'm not from here."

"But – it's all over the news. Don't you keep up with politics, Tom?"

"Not really…"

"Well I suppose it's easy for me to say – it's kind of an occupational hazard for me." She shrugged her ample shoulders. "Radiakka II is where they want to expand the Radiakkan Empire. They want to continue to grow and extend across the galaxy."

"Where is Radiakka II?"

"Well that's just it – the Radiakkan government haven't told anyone yet. I thought we could pretend we were on a mission to find out."

Tom thought about this for a moment.

"That sounds like it could be tricky, Gracer. If it's supposed to be top secret, then we're not going to be able to find out." A torrent of recollection of discovering the truth about Truxxe lurched through his memory like a wave of sickness. He had enough to worry about, he knew, although he *had* to admit that he was intrigued.

"Oh, we won't find out, Tom. I told you – it's just for fun! It's just an excuse to have a nose around really. I don't get much chance, usually, holed up in my office."

Tom didn't quite understand Gracer's way of thinking. She seemed to have a strange way of looking at the world.

"Right – so, tell me more about this. Does the government want a similar world to this one? Another hot spot for holiday makers?"

"Oh no, not initially. They made that mistake with Radiakka I." Gracer said matter-of-factly. "They'll want to use it for colonisation. They'll want to invade."

"Invade?" Tom stopped for a moment. They were halfway along a long, red lit corridor. "What do you mean? How do you know this?"

A group of muttering suit-wearers brushed past them rather rudely.

"It's just the most likely method they'll use. Why land on a barren planet and build up from scratch? They'll find somewhere with a thriving settlement and take over, I expect."

Tom gulped. Perhaps the Radiakkan culture was not the best race to be interfering with. "Maybe we should leave this one, Gracer."

"What? Don't be silly, we're near the offices now. We'll just need to hack into a computer and have a look. Wouldn't it be great to find out which planet they're planning on?... Uh oh."

Uh oh? That doesn't sound good.

Suddenly, Gracer dropped to the floor. She was clutching her stomach.

"Quickly, get some help!" she croaked.

"What? Gracer – are you OK?" he knelt down beside her.

Two indigo skinned creatures who had been walking along the corridor stopped and stared.

"Yes!" she hissed into his ear. "Call for one of the doctors!"

Tom guessed that Gracer was pretending. If she was reaching for this planet's equivalent of an Oscar, she would at least be a nominee. The strange creature was giving a convincing performance.

"Help!" She called out.

"OK, OK!" Tom played along.

He had an idea.

He spoke into his timepiece.

"Frarkk – Frarkk can you hear me?"

"Tom – where are you? Have you found anything?"

"You could say that – Frarkk I think your er… ahem… *doctor* skills are needed. Try and get a premium pass so that you can get into the long corridor off the staff canteen." Tom explained in hushed tones that Gracer was playing as another decoy so that he could sneak into the office and have a look at the computer files. Tom then realised that his skills as a hacker were not going to win him any prizes.

"And Frarkk – bring Hyganty with you!"

Tom stayed with Gracer, a hand resting gently on her shoulder.

"Help is on the way," he reassured her and winked. She didn't wink back. Perhaps the ALSID unit here wasn't translating the gesture. The two indigo-skinned beings bent down in unison to take a closer look at the fallen employee.

"Don't worry, she'll be fine," Tom told them.

"We were not worrying!" they both snapped. They looked at each other with their large goggle eyes and then continued on their journey.

"Outsiders!" One of them muttered.

"What was their problem?" Tom looked at Gracer. Her gills were pulsating quickly. She really was playing the part well.

# **CHAPTER 17**

Nathan Reed was practising his spotoon skills on the far wall of cell 7A. It didn't seem fair that he'd come all this way to see Tom and he'd gone off to yet another planet without him. Even this cell was more pleasant than his home on Earth at the moment. No mess, no moaning father and three meals a day which he didn't have to cook. He sighed.

A pherobot guard appeared in the doorway, seemingly grinning at him through its grill. Nathan automatically stood up. He brushed himself down and stood up straight, hoping that the saliva dripping down the wall did not disgust the beautiful android.

"You're free to go, prisoner 7A," she chimed.

"Free? What? Really?" Nathan did not know what to say.

It clanked up to him.

"We do not have any evidence that you know anything about the Truxxian Raphyl's case, so we have no reason to hold you any longer. By way of apology for any inconvenience caused, we would like to offer you a free trip home in our luxury transporter craft. Unfortunately, our data bank containing your details has been corrupted, therefore please could you state your location of origin?"

"My location of origin?" Nathan scratched his unshaven chin, thoughtfully. He grinned. "Take me back home to Radiakka!"

Tom could make out the insect-like frames of Frarkk and Hyganty at the far end of the corridor. They had evidently managed to acquire premium passes, owing to Frarkk's doctor guise. The two had been escorted to the situation by one of the robotic guides – a pathetic attempt at security, in Tom's opinion.

Gracer's eyes were closed and she was still breathing rapidly. Several people, office workers and security staff, had come out of their respective rooms. They were standing around, murmuring incoherently amongst themselves.

Consequently, the room Tom needed to get to was now clear of parliamentary personnel. Tom had noticed that none of the concerned staff had been Radiakkans, however. All of the native men which he'd seen emerging had shrugged their shoulders, muttered something about caffeine shots and left in the direction of the canteen. Tom found their behaviour most odd.

"I'm here, now. Please let me through, everyone," announced Frarkk. As Frarkk made his way towards the "patient", Tom began to weave through the crowd to the office door which was ajar. Hyganty ducked into the room with him, unseen by the gathering.

The office was much larger than Tom had imagined. Stretching at least twelve metres by ten, it was carpeted in lavish crimson red with walls adorned with more of those odd portraits that Tom had encountered in the entrance hall. He found himself staring at the paintings and found that he was getting transfixed by them again. He had to force himself to look away. A desk the size of a family dining table was home to a bank of computer terminals. Hyganty was already tapping away at one of the keyboards. Tom loved computers, but he was more of a gamer than a hacker. Plus, he suspected that the systems used here would be more complicated than the simple touch screens in the TSS express cuisine.

He left Hyganty to work his magic and walked over to the window. The city had a beautiful skyline. The relentless sun was reflecting off the ornate roof of the Office of Victory and the surrounding structures. The street was peppered with a spectrum of blossoming plants, pink, yellow, aqua, indigo. His eyes then fell to the street level and he watched as another Tops Tours bus pulled up, brimming with another batch of sightseers. Tom wondered how far the tour group they'd arrived with had journeyed through the building and what delights Kayleesh was being confronted with. He chuckled to himself. He knew she'd be bursting with speculation.

There was a sudden furore outside in the corridor.

"Hyganty, what's happening?"

"Wait a krom. I'm almost there…" Hyganty said without looking away from the screen.

"What have you found?" Tom asked urgently. "Is it about Radiakka II?"

"How did you know about that?" Hyganty looked discomfited, as though a huge praying mantis in clothing, crouching to work on a computer designed for humanoids didn't look awkward enough. "I've found what we need. I just need to transfer the data to this disc and we're ready to go."

Hyganty flashed a plastic card, much like the ones Tom used in his melody mech back on Truxxe.

There was a distinctive scream out in the corridor.

Gracer?

"Hyganty!" he called, quickly

Hyganty waved a pincer at him, indicating that he was still otherwise engaged.

Tom made for the door, surprised by his own bravery. He creaked it open, but the crowd was obscuring his view. What was happening? Was someone hurting her? Something must be happening, or the horde would have surely dwindled by now.

Another scream.

"Tom!" Gracer spotted Tom as he pushed his way through the crowd. She had stopped screaming. In fact, she was smiling. She was sitting up, perspiration on her brow. In her lap she was clutching a large egg.

Schlomm Putt was in sector thirteen. It didn't look much like a gambling hall. In fact, it looked more like a laundrette. A very busy, noisy laundrette. Sentry One Four One's shoulders fell in dismay. Glorbians didn't even do washing.

The walls of the room were stacked high with rumbling machines and pipes ran around the ceiling. One Four One felt as though he were in the belly of a giant beast which was digesting tonnes of laundry – and a dozen prison workers besides. Some were heaving taupe piles of uniforms into machines; others were carrying sodden mounds through a door labelled driers; while others were folding sheets, in pairs.

A guard, whose number was obscured by a towering pile of uniforms, bumbled past him. A pile of underwear came at him from the opposite direction, causing the small Glorbian to spin round.

"Do you mind?" he said, crossly.

"Can I help you, One Four One?" A small voice tweeted, politely.

One Four One looked around him, searching for the source of the voice.

"Down here."

Schlomm was surprised to find someone who was smaller than himself standing at his feet. A pink-skinned, feline-featured creature blinked at him.

"I'm afraid that we can't wash clothes that you are still wearing, One Four One."

"What do you mean?" Schlomm scowled. The real One Four One's uniform was the cleanest item of clothing ever to have had the misfortune to have accommodated Schlomm's body. He brushed himself down. By his standards, the uniform was immaculate. But then, Glorbians didn't have very high standards.

"Apologies, One Four One," the cat creature paused. "Unless you're here for - never mind..."

"You mean I *have* found the right place?" Schlomm's grin widened and a globule of spit landed on the creature's head. It hissed, instinctively, before leaping up onto what he thought might be One Four One's shoulder. Schlomm couldn't see what number was adorned on his little uniform. He was either too low down or too close to see and Schlomm did not feel like going out of his way to find out if the answer was not already evident. The small life form leaned over and whispered into where it suspected One Four One's ear might be.

"Follow me."

"How can I follow you if you if you're on my shoulder?"

"Good point," it chirruped. "All right then, make your way to the drying room. Go to the far end and around the corner to the large drier which says, *out of order.*"

The Glorbian did as he was instructed. The door to the drying room hummed open to disclose a smaller, L-shaped room. There was indeed a drier which appeared to be out of service.

"Well, go on then," a voice all but pierced his ear drum.

"Go on, what?"

"Step inside!"

The Glorbian peeled the creature off his shoulder and held him in front of his face.

"Now why would I want to do that?"

"Trust me. Step inside the drier!"

"I don't trust you as far as I could… swing you," he spat.

"Fine, it's up to you, your loss. But please put me down. I've got pillows to plump."

One Four One let him go in mid-air, narrowing his eyes as the feline landed gracefully on the floor on four legs and then slinked away on two.

*What is fish breath talking about?*

One Four One went to walk away but noticed that this part of the room was empty. There would be no one to watch his blunder if this was a trick. He scratched his chin. He looked around him once more, opened the door to the drier and peered inside.

"Perfect!"

# CHAPTER 18

People were clapping and cheering and voicing their congratulations. Frarkk helped Gracer to her feet and gave a demi bow for the onlookers. The assembly clapped a while longer, then soon began to dissipate. This was one of the most bizarre sights Tom Bowler had ever witnessed. He couldn't keep his eye off the egg in Gracer's arms.

"I thought you were pretending!"

"Where did you get that idea?" Gracer was rocking her egg, now.

"You said – you said that you were OK."

"I *was* OK, Tom. I knew what was happening, but that doesn't mean I was pretending. I'm sorry if I shocked you."

"It's not your fault… it's OK," Tom smiled. "Wow. An egg!" He was bewildered.

"I'm glad that you called for Frarkk, here."

"Frarkk, have you done this kind of thing before?" Tom asked.

"No, but I've a feeling that if I'd left you in charge you would have fainted."

"Hey!" Tom protested. "Actually – you're probably right."

"Right, well thanks, guys." Gracer patted the encased infant with affection. "I'll go and put him with the others."

"Others?" said Tom and Frarkk in unison.

Hyganty presently joined the stunned pair in the corridor. He didn't seem to notice that the little decoy party had disappeared.

"We've definitely chosen the right building. Of all the buildings that ACD designed in their lifetime, we've picked the right one!"

"The right one? Wouldn't Porriduum be the right one?" Frarkk asked.

Hyganty's time piece lit up before he could answer.

"Where are you all?" It was Kayleesh's voice.

*What was she doing calling him? She could just as easily have called me!*

"Kayleesh, we're all together. Have you finished the tour?"

"No – I stuck with it as long as I could, but," her voice dropped to a whisper. Tom could just about make out her words. "Radiakkan history is all very interesting – but it's a bit self-righteous, a bit nationalistic. There was only so much I could take! So, I managed to slip away during the lunch break out in the grounds. Meet me by the small coppice out the back of the building. But be quick – I'm hiding up a tree!"

"That bad, eh?" Tom roared with laughter.

Kayleesh climbed gracefully down from the tree and landed next to the others.

"Well?"

Tom sniggered. He knew that Kayleesh would be desperate to discover Hyganty's findings. He was too, of course, but the delightful Augtopian amused him.

They were in a thicket at the far end of a long, ornamental garden. The tourist group were back by the main building by now. The garden reminded Tom of the grounds of a castle Tom had visited on a school trip, minus the peacock calls and jobbing thespians dressed as jousting knights and dancing damsels. Flowers of many varieties were arranged in patterns on the immense lawn. Statues stood proud, slick and flawless and water trickled into a nearby pond from a fountain in the shape of a Wheylandian warrior. The sound of the fountain awakened Tom's bladder. He tried his best to ignore the urge.

Hyganty sat down on the cool grass. The rest followed suit. Tom was sitting opposite Hyganty and realised that the insect was looking over his shoulder. Tom craned his neck round. Was there someone behind him?

No, only the watery warrior.

Perhaps the noise was affecting Hyganty's bladder too. When he looked back, however, the Submian was looking down at his plastic card, rolling it between his pincers.

"From thoroughly searching through the system's data banks, I have managed to acquire some very interesting encrypted information. The files haven't even been accessed in at least two lifetimes."

"And you managed to de-code it?" Kayleesh grinned.

"Of course." One of Hyganty's feelers caressed the plastic card. "Not only are we at the right building – we're almost at the right spot."

"Right spot for what?" Tom asked.

"The information in the computer data bank holds the truth about the whereabouts of Raghael and Mirrie, Raphyl's parents."

"The whereabouts?" said Kayleesh. "You mean their graves?"

"Not their graves."

"Their ashes, then? They've been dead for hundreds of years!"

"You need to look at it laterally," Hyganty pointed at each of them with the plastic card, a teacher's pointy stick. "Raghael and Mirrie received an award for their contribution to this building - correct? Well, I don't think that their architectural skills are their only contribution to this building."

"What are you saying, Hyganty?" Frarkk was as puzzled as any of them.

"Look around you – what do you see?"

"Trees, grass, flowers, a fountain, more flowers, statues," Kayleesh shrugged.

"Statues, yes!" reiterated Hyganty. "However, not all of them are statues."

"What do you mean?" Tom's eyes narrowed. His thoughts began to wander around his brain. If they weren't statues, what were they? Strange looking plants? Street performers? Very slow-moving aliens? In fact, he was nearly there with that last thought.

"Do you all remember when we were in Raphyl's apartment and we found that three-hundred-year-old newspaper?"

"Of course," Kayleesh said with frustration in her voice, practically about to detonate. "Oh, come on Hyganty, tell us!"

"And do you remember how we reflected on the possibility of Raphyl having spent all that time in cryo? Well, from the data I received, I've reason to believe that Raphyl did not kill his parents. He didn't kill them because they're not dead. They're in cryo too. And this disc is the key – it contains vital components of their personalities. They cannot be awakened successfully without it."

"Awakened? If you're right, Hyganty," said Frarkk. "Then, that disc is the only way we can release the evidence of Raphyl's innocence!"

"But what about the statues?" Kayleesh exploded.

"I said to think laterally, dear Augtopian. According to the recovered data, there are a pair of statues round here that do a little more than just resemble this building's architects!"

"You mean that Raghael and Mirrie are here? Their bodies are frozen here, in the grounds - for all to see?"

Hyganty nodded. On a scale of one to ten of smugness, the Submian was emitting a solid twelve.

"Where?" Tom looked about him. Was this why Hyganty had been peering over his shoulder? Had he been scanning the area for the petrified Truxxians?

"We'll need to find them in the grounds. I can't use this disc as evidence that Raphyl's parents were never murdered – not unless I wanted to be on the wrong side of the bars on Porriduum. The legal system would not look kindly on illegal information retrieval – especially from Radiakka."

Tom's thoughts were pacing again. They pulled the light bulb cord in his head.

"So, we need hard evidence – we need to find out how to wake up Raghael and Mirrie."

"Indeed we do," said Hyganty.

The group had waited in the coppice until sunset; until the last of the visitors and departed; until the last chocolate bar wrapper had been sucked up by the last hovering, hoovering bot. They had snuck around the perimeter of the grounds, searching for the figurines of Raphyl's parents, ducking out of the way of security cameras. Tom supposed that Gracer would have loved such an adventure, creeping around the garden like a spy. He wondered how she was. Was she tending to her clutch of eggs? No wonder she had to eat so much – she had to replenish so much energy. But he couldn't tell Gracer what they were really doing. She worked in the Parliamentary Building so it would be far too risky. Tom had enjoyed hiding in the woods, huddled beside Kayleesh; the scent of her tingling his senses; her closeness.

If they had been alone, maybe he would have made a move. Maybe.

Tom Bowler tapped the cold, hard stone of his friend's mother's likeness. Both statues bore resemblance to the newspaper clipping photograph of the Truxxian couple but looked so lifeless that it was hard to image that they were anything more than just statues. *Perhaps that's the idea,* pondered Tom. He walked a figure of eight around the pair; his eyes scanning for some kind of clue. A button? An auto-defrost setting? What was he looking for?

"Open Sesame!" Tom boomed and grinned.

"Keep your voice down!" Frarkk warned, predictably missing
the joke.

"Hyganty, were there any clues on the data file?" Kayleesh asked, after she had circled Mirrie for the fourth time. "I'm not sure what we should be looking for."

"I didn't have much time to read all the details – getting them loaded onto this card was my priority at the time," Hyganty paused and rubbed his chin with a feeler. "You have a point though Kayleesh – I'll make my way back to the ship and plug the card into my console. There's not a lot you can all do here at the moment. There's no obvious way of releasing the Truxxians that I can see."

"Is there *nothing* we can do?" whined Kayleesh.
"You might as well just make the most of your visit. It's still quite early.. I'm sure there are plenty of night spots you could visit in Wheyland."

"If you're going Hyganty, then you'll have to go now to be able to make the last tour bus," warned Frarkk. "In fact, I'll come with you. Let's leave the young ones to it. We can pick them up later."

Tom smiled, inwardly. Alone with Kayleesh at last.

# CHAPTER 19

The Glorbian space pirate Schlomm, currently disguised as Sentry One Four One, stepped out of the doorway, which was currently disguised as a tumble drier. One of the oddest sights Schlomm had ever seen lay before him - and Schlomm had witnessed some odd scenes in his time.

Masked by the sound of the noisy laundry complex next door, this room was buzzing with more activity than a Glorbian glee hive. Schlomm could sense the energy generated by the room to his very toes; the excitement, the anticipation, the to-ing and fro-ing of coins; and all under the very noses of the prison guards. In fact, it was *run* by prison guards and even their customers were prison guards. Schlomm rubbed his feet together with delight. The strangest aspect about the room was that the air was moist - there was more steam in here than in the laundry room itself. In fact, Schlomm construed that the steam from the laundry room was in fact being pumped into this room. He craned what he passed as a neck and saw that most of the steam looked as though it was being channelled through transparent pipes across the ceiling. The conduits routed the steam to half a dozen tables which were stationed around the room. Schlomm tried to make sense of it all. He padded over to one of the tables and observed. Six gamblers were jostling around it, their eyes - and other viewing appendages – fixed on the central focus of the table: a single windowpane.

He spotted sentry Nine, one of the humanoids he'd met in the canteen. He was leaping around like a Spotoon cheerleader.

"Come on number nine! Only five inches to go. You can do it!"

Schlomm followed Nine's gaze. He appeared to be watching the progression of a raindrop. The Glorbian's mouth was so full of questions that he had to open it before they came spewing out in the wrong order. But before any of his words could link themselves coherently, Nine bounded into the air, whooping with glee. He turned to a startled Truxxian next to him and kissed him.

"Yes!" Nine punched the air. Or at least a human being under the influence of the station's ALSID would have translated it that way. What he actually did was too disgusting to print.

"Congratulations," Schlomm said.

"Sentry One Four One!" Nine enthused, beads of energised sweat dancing on his pale brow. "I'm glad you managed to find us, Glorbian! I trust that you're going to have a wager?"

"Have I got this correct?" Schlomm eyed the excited creature. He thought him a mad fool. A rich mad fool now, perhaps. "You have just placed a bet on which water droplet will reach the bottom of the window-pane on the desk?"

"That's right – the most exciting sport in the complex. What makes it more exciting is the fact that it's prohibited. And today the most exciting part about it is that I've won – not only that but I've won a lot!"

"Quite," Schlomm raised an eyebrow. "But what I can't understand is – why are you talking to me when there's a pile of money waiting for you to collect?"

"Good point! Come with me while I collect it and I'll tell you my secret."

If there was an offer that Schlomm could not refuse, it was this one. He followed Sentry Nine to a desk at the far end of the room. There was another whoop of joy from one of the other tables. Schlomm eyed the cashier; a Strellion. Not best positioned in such an establishment – Strellions were famous for being untrustworthy and deceitful. He wondered how a Strellion had even got a job on Porriduum in the first place. Perhaps it was part of the equal opportunities and diversity act.

"Table A, droplet number Nine," beamed Nine. The Strellion nodded and held out two rubber bungs.

"A multiplier. Congratulations, Nine. Do you want me to put these on the next game? Table C is will be ready for another in ten kroms."

"No, I'll take them now. I don't want anyone getting too suspicious," Nine winked. He grabbed the bungs, greedily. The Strellion, sentry One Five Six, tapped his distended nose, knowingly. These people looked harmless enough; cuddly, fluffy and corpulent. But a Strellion, as most folk knew, may look like the innocent bloom, but in fact be the coiled Lueanian river snake under it.

"I think our colleague here would like to place a bet, however." Nine winked again. "He has the necessary funds."

Schlomm did not like anyone knowing his business, particularly when it was related to money, but if it was a means for him to gain *more* money, then he allowed himself to permit it.

"Could we use table C then?" Nine continued. "And we'll have the er... *drip plus.*"

"Of course – I wouldn't have expected you to have gambled on an *ordinary* drip, Sentry Nine."

*"Drip plus?"* re-iterated Schlomm.

"Hand over your shrapnel and I'll tell you," Nine promised. Schlomm bundled the coin bags onto the counter. He eyed the Strellion who promptly placed each bag onto a pair of scales and peered inside each one to check their contents.

"All seems well," the tender smiled. "Your drip will be ready in five kroms – number seven."

Nine steered the Glorbian into a corner of the room. He had ceased perspiring, but still had the look of an excited infant about him.

"Why don't I get to choose my own drop? I don't like being told what to do, particularly by a Strellion," Schlomm harrumphed.

"Because you've chosen *drip plus* of course!"

"Please explain. And I had better win this because I just handed all of my er... available cash over to that suspicious looking Strellion!"

"You're right to be concerned," the pale humanoid nodded. "But the point is that you will win."

One Four One harrumphed again.

"You see the steam which is being pumped through the conduits? Well, One Five Six is in the back room programming the nanobots for your game as we speak. They are the *plus* in your *drip plus,* of course."

*"Nanobots?"*

"Yes, tiny programmable robots – smaller than the eye can see –"

"Yes, I know what nanobots are, you fool. But how will they help me?"

"One Five Six will insert a small army of dormant nanobots into the pocket of one of the uniforms in the laundry which he'll then ask an assistant to put through the speed wash. The water will bring the nanobots out of hibernation. They will have a direct route from the machine, along the steam conduits and to the pane on the game table. The clever part is that they will then proceed to convert the water droplet to alcohol by removing a hydrogen atom from each molecule. This will make it a thinner substance than water and therefore the drip will run down the pane at a faster pace than the H2O droplets. With the extra hydrogen, they will have fuel enough to not only power themselves, but to propel the drip further."

"Sounds complicated," Schlomm admitted.

"But it works. It's a very subtle, but very effective method."

Schlomm's grin widened. "Is that how you won that last game?"

"Of course. And the three games previous."

Schlomm observed the other gamblers in the room. One was cheering with delight, revelling in triumph. Another was hanging his head in defeat. Schlomm decided that he was going to be the former.

Tom Bowler was finally alone with Kayleesh. One problem which hadn't occurred to him, however, was communication. He found communication with girls difficult at the best of times, but once he and Kayleesh were out of the vicinity of the Parliamentary Building and grounds, he realised that there was no ALSID within range They were walking along pretty lane lined by street lamps and trees in full bloom. He didn't know where they were going. He was just happy to be near her. He had tried to speak, but Kayleesh's reaction had indicated that the ALSID influence had faded. Perhaps he could show a friendly gesture which didn't require words. Perhaps he could hold her hand. His hand twitched Kayleeshwards, but then he dropped it to his side again. What if the action didn't mean anything to her, without an ALSID to translate it? What if she took it as a hostile move? *Would it translate it at all?* It was times like this that Tom wished things were simpler. He had had girlfriends in the past, but he had never felt like this about any of them. Not really. None of them were as inquisitive, adventurous, intelligent or half as pretty - even if she was an alien. And that was the other problem. She may find him as repulsive as he found a Glorbian. He sighed.

They soon happened upon a building. An amber glow spilled onto the pavement; light music tumbled out of the windows Tom believed that they had stumbled upon a public house.

"Shall we go inside?" Kayleesh asked.

The building must have an ALSID! Tom nodded.

# CHAPTER 20

Tom felt as though the two of them could quite easily be in a bar at a tropical holiday destination back on Earth - save for the lively indigo creatures who were propping up the bar. Tall, leafy plants were dotted here and there, and the amber lighting complimented the plush decor. It wasn't as busy as bar Six Seven on Truxxe, and there were fewer aliens. In fact, Tom realised that he and Kayleesh were the only Non-Radiakkan patrons. Kayleesh found a table she liked the look of and promptly sat down. She rubbed an aching foot, as girls do after a walk of more than half a mile in ridiculous shoes. Tom noticed that he and Kayleesh weren't the only outsiders, another human was walking back from the bar, holding a brimming glass. And it wasn't just any human. It was Nathan.

Completely dismissing previous thoughts of alone time with Kayleesh, Tom vaulted over a vacant chair and landed in front of his friend.

"Once again I find you in a pub on a strange planet," Tom laughed. "What are you *doing* here?"

"Looking for you."

"Yes, it really looks that way," Tom raised an eyebrow as Nathan sipped his drink, froth clinging to his stubble.

"I was! What is your excuse anyway? Oh!" Nathan had spotted the back of Kayleesh's head. "Well I can leave you to it if you like."

"No, don't be silly, bud. You're here now and I probably shouldn't lose you again. Come and sit with us."

Tom continued on to the bar and returned with a lager for himself and a glass of Augtopian Vapore. Kayleesh was laughing.

"Nathan's just been telling me how he got here. Ingenious, really."

"That's our Nathan," Tom sipped his drink as Nathan told him how he had managed to get transported to Radiakka, by falsely informing the security on TSS that this was his home-planet, as they had lost his details. He told them how pleased he was to be free again. "It was a bit of a risk, though – what if we had left by the time you got here? Then you'd be stranded!"

"I was pretty much stranded anyway, Bud. And anyway, I like a risk!"

"Are you sure you didn't break out, Nathan?"

"What, and hijack a spaceship to here? Even *I* couldn't do something that crazy. Speaking of breaking out - any progress on rescuing Raphyl?" Tom informed Nathan of the day's exploits: strange paintings, alien eggs and statues included. Nathan seemed impressed. "That's quite a busy day you've had. And here I was thinking you were wasting the entire time in the nearest bar you could find!"

"I think you and Raphyl would get on very well," Kayleesh observed, twirling her empty glass in her fingers.

"Empty glasses?" Nathan gasped. "We can't have empty glasses!" he swiftly jumped up and headed for the bar.

"Very well," said Kayleesh.

"You know, what this place needs is a Spotoon board," Nathan slurred, several drinks later.

Tom nodded. He hadn't played the sport for a few days. "I wonder if they have one?"

Before Tom had even finished his sentence, Nathan had made another pilgrimage to the bar, apparently to enquire.

"What?" Tom heard the barman bellow. "That vulgar sport was banned from Radiakka generations ago!" Nathan must have made a further comment, although Tom couldn't hear him over the bar room chatter, as the barman's next retort was even more raucous. "How dare you question our ways? I knew we should never have had the ALSID unit installed – it encourages undesirables! Now get out of my establishment before I set the guard bot onto you – all three of you!"

Nathan appeared at the table again, a sheepish look on his face.

"I know, I heard," Tom sighed. "Come on then, let's go."

"Strange race, aren't they?" Nathan mused once they were on the friendlier side of the doorway.

"Think about it, bud. They don't exactly allow the game on Earth either, do they?"

"Well he didn't have to be so rude about it – throwing us out like that. All I said was that they were narrow-minded and…"

But the influence of the ALSID unit wore off and only Tom could understand the end of his sentence. He shook his head, laughing. Nathan was back.

Schlomm Putt was sweating with nervous anticipation. He had the loaded drip seven in his sight. If it won, then he would be absolutely exultant. If it lost, then all he had really lost was some currency stolen from a real prison guard's stolen uniform. Even so, the prospect of losing disconcerted him. He hoped that the pale humanoid was telling the truth. Nine joined him at his side.

"It looks like the nanobots are at work!"

"Yes, drip seven does seem to be speeding up," the grumpy-faced Schlomm almost squealed with delight. Almost. The Glorbian held his breath in anticipation as the droplet descended the pane. He didn't realise he was doing this until he started to feel dizzy and wondered why his vision was blurring. Breathe Schlomm, you need to be conscious when drip seven wins. Another drip was catching up, and its Truxxian gambler shuffled around excitedly on the other side of the table. But drip seven gained a little more speed as it was propelled to the end of its racetrack in first position. Schlomm grinned.

Tom, Nathan and Kayleesh were walking idly back in the direction of the Submian ship. At least, Tom and Kayleesh were following the road, retracing the route of the tour bus as best as they could remember. Nathan's path was a little more wobbly, due to the amount of Radiakkan beer he had consumed.

"I thought they were going to pick you up…" Nathan began, jabbing a finger in the air, drunkenly, and almost missing his footing. "…in their big spaceship thingy."

"Yes, but they don't know where we're going to be, do they? And they can't land in these narrow streets. It's a shame we've got to leave so soon, but it doesn't look like we're welcome anywhere where there is an ALSID, thanks to someone not a million miles away from me!"

"Not any more I'm not!" Nathan quipped and laughed loudly, giving his friend a heavy pat on the shoulder. Tom laughed too.

"We may as well make our way back. I hate not being able to talk to Kayleesh."

"I bet she's glad of the rest," Nathan jibed.

The banter between the two of them continued for half a mile or so. Kayleesh, alone on account of the language barrier, was apparently humming away to herself quite happily as they walked.

The Submian ship landed fifty yards away in front of them. Nathan gaped.

"I've made a discovery," Hyganty announced as the three of them walked onto the bridge. "I've worked through of all the encrypted data on this card and it seems that we are able to disable the cryo state of the Truxxians. This disc now actually contains the activation codes for the statues. Their personalities, as it were."

"How strange! So, the personalities of Raphyl's mum and dad were saved onto a computer?" Kayleesh gasped.

"If that's true then what do we do with the disc?" Tom asked. "How do we get the information off it and back into Raphyl's frozen parents? There weren't any slots on the base of the statues or anything from what I remember. No device. There was nothing. They just looked like… stone!"

"You're right. There was nothing visible above ground." Hyganty stroked his chin with a feeler.

"You mean there might be a way underneath the figures?" said Kayleesh.

"According to the data downloaded from the computer."

"I just knew there were secret passageways," grinned Tom.

# CHAPTER 21

Nathan was enjoying himself aboard the Submian ship. Hyganty was giving him and Tom a tour. They were turning down one khaki-coloured corridor after another, occasionally dipping into rooms which led off the passageways.

"It's even more impressive than the Truxxe transit I arrived in. I could fly one of these!" Nathan expressed.

"Oh, you think so, do you? It's challenge enough staying sane while this thing takes off, let alone actually piloting it." Tom warned.

"And it's a damn sight bigger than the pod I was abducted in." He whistled, clearly impressed.

Hyganty stopped and indicated a nearby doorway with a pincer. "If you'd like to rest, you can use this room. Tom, you can use the room next door."

"Why thanks, bud!" Nathan grinned and accepted the Submian's offer by instantly entering the room and throwing himself straight onto a bunk. "Night then!" He waved a hand as the bedroom door was sliding closed.

"You didn't need to ask him twice," laughed Tom. "I may as well get some rest too."

"Very well. You'll need some sleep before tomorrow's shift at the Parliamentary Building."

"What? This is my weekend off – I'm not going back there again," Tom moaned.

"Your cover as a work experience employee will still be viable. The person you replaced may be back in action tomorrow, but you still have your pass."

*"His* pass," Tom corrected him.

"They won't know that. We'll talk about it tomorrow." Hyganty withdrew to the bridge.

"Yes, mum," muttered Tom.

The room was a simple affair, offering a bedside table, a closet and a small adjoining room which Tom assumed was the sanitation section. His bladder was screaming so he was relieved, quite literally, to discover that the small room was indeed equipped with some manner of a toilet bowl and a tub with a shower head.

Throughout his shower, he was still muttering to himself about Hyganty's officious behaviour. When he had finished, he saw that Kayleesh was sitting on his bunk. His heart caught in his throat. She was giggling, which saw to only melt his heart which slid back into its rightful place. What was she doing in his quarters? Perhaps she'd absorbed too much Augtopian Vapore. That would definitely account for the giggling.

He said hello and pulled himself onto the bunk next to her.

"Hi Tom. I was too excited to sleep, and I thought I'd come and talk to you. I hope you don't mind."

"Mind? Of course not. Any time. Do you want to talk about the 'Truxxian disc adventure' or the 'Release Raphyl expedition'?" Tom laughed.

Kayleesh looked quizzical. "Neither really, to be truthful. And aren't they both part of the same quest? Anyway, I was in my quarters thinking about my home world and I got a little melancholy."

"Augtopia?"

Kayleesh nodded. "I remember when you used the holoceiver to communicate with your family back on Earth. I've never done that from TSS."

"Really? Why don't you?"

"I may have mentioned before that my dad doesn't approve of me working on Truxxe. He had other plans for me."

"Other plans?"

"Yes, he wanted me to continue on the family business."

"I see. What kind of business is that?" Tom shuffled a little closer to her. The bunk was quite comfortable. He made an effort to listen to Kayleesh, despite what his body was telling him to do.

"They er… my parents are er… well, they're performing artists."

"Impressive! Are they in a band?"

"No," Kayleesh said nervously.

"OK. A theatre group?"

"Not… exactly." Kayleesh bit her lip. She paused a good few seconds. "They're part of a circus. A travelling freak show, to be precise."

*"A freak show?"*

"Don't look so surprised. I thought you may have guessed."

"How could I have guessed?" Tom was drowning in an ocean of bewilderment. "What do you mean?"

"Well, maybe you won't have guessed. That's partly the reason for my moving away from Augtopia - so that no one would know otherwise. But I still feel like a freak."

"In what way are you a freak? You… you're *perfect!*"

"That's not true, Tom." Kayleesh sighed. She wiped a tear from her eye; her beautiful, violet, almond-shaped eye. "My whole family suffers from deformities. My father has uncontrollable bodily hair growth, as does my sister…" Tom bit the inside of his cheek to prevent himself from laughing at the mental image of which his mind was cruelly taunting him. It would be exceptionally inconsiderate of him to laugh while the object of his affections was confiding in him. "And my mother and I… my mother and I have… tiny chins." Kayleesh's inner damn gave way and water came flooding out of those violet eyes. Tom instinctively put an arm around her shoulders.

"Tiny chins? But your chin is -"

"- perfect, according to you. I know," she finished, voice quivering. "But where I come from, this is not normal." She jabbed at her chiselled jaw line.

"So, in that case I must look like a freak to you," Tom said.

"No, of course not -"

"Honestly, it's nothing to get upset about. As you said, I wouldn't have known if that was 'normal' where you come from or not and even if you did have a big chin – look I'm getting myself tied up in knots here … what I really mean to say is-"

"There's a huge swarm of carnivorous dragonflies making their way onto the bridge." Tom's timepiece burst into life.

# CHAPTER 22

Sentry One Four One, Schlomm Putt, allowed himself a merry jig as his third bet in a row thrusted his internal happy metre into the astral plain. That is to say, his grumpy metre was utterly empty for the first time in years. Hardly seeing the other gamblers through his rapturous daze, the Glorbian made his way to the counter and met with the Strellion.

"I'd like to collect my winnings, please," he said smugly.

"Congratulations, One Four One." The Strellion winked at him. "Three consecutive wins have earned you seven bungs." Schlomm bore all of his yellow teeth in their full glory in a disturbing grin. Hands outstretched, he awaited his prize. "But what's this? A Glorbian is giving in? Surely not," said the Strellion.

"What?"

"You're not stopping now, when you're doing so well are you?"

"Are you saying that I should stake another bet?"

"I'm saying it'd be a crime not too. Just one more wager will *double* your winnings." He leant closer to the vertically-challenged Glorbian. "And you know that you cannot possibly lose."

"Ahem, very well." Schlomm pulled himself up to his full three feet of height. "I'd like to place my money on another bet. *All of it.*"

"Sentry, you do realise this is a guaranteed win?"

"I expect it to be true, yes. With the old er... *drip plus,*" he whispered with a wink.

"Then for maximum pay-out, you might want to consider placing a higher stake."

"A higher stake? But this is all the money I have!"

"Oh, it doesn't have to be money. If you were to use something else, a spaceship for example, you could find yourself walking away with an even bigger prize."

*"A bigger prize?"* Schlomm's eyes twinkled, greedily. What could be bigger than a spaceship? "You mean, bigger as in a... *planet?"*

"Well let's not get too far ahead of ourselves, One Four One. I was thinking bigger as in maybe a *prisoner transporter ship."*

Schlomm pondered. It would be much simpler to smuggle Hannond off Porriduum in an actual prisoner transporter ship than use the compositor device on the Cluock again. He smiled.

"I have a Glorbian goods transporter spacecraft in my possession. Would that be a worthy bet?"

"Oh, very worthy indeed, sir."

Hannond Putt's cell mate was snoring loudly. He rolled onto his back, sighing and grumbling to himself. *Shut up, shut up!* He eventually decided to admit defeat, gave an even bigger sigh and sat up. As he did so he noticed a spherical object hanging in the air. What is that? How mysterious. How beautiful! Hannond had the advantage of the top bunk, so he clambered to a standing position and patted at the air with his hands in an attempt to reach the bubble. The snoring was unrelenting.

Hannond reached out as far as he could from his position on the top bunk. The thumb of his right hand finally caught the edge of the bubble. Hannond gasped in disgust as his vision of the tantalising sphere was exchanged for a breath of putrid gas and stinging eyes. The stench was unbearable.

"There's a what?" Kayleesh shrieked.

"There's a huge swarm of carnivorous dragonflies making their way onto the bridge!" Frarkk's disembodied voice reiterated.

"Did you say *carnivorous?"* Tom gaped. He thought about mosquitoes on Earth. Were they carnivorous? *They do bite, but then they eat nectar so maybe they're omnivores,* he wondered. Perhaps Frarkk is overreacting. "Haven't you got any bug spray on board?"

"The situation is beyond *bug spray,* as you put it," Frarkk paused. "We'll have to use the ship's internal defence system to smoke them out."

"Smoke them out? OK well then we'll just wait in here until they've all gone."

"It's not that simple. The defence system has been offline for so long that Hyganty will have to work on it before it can be activated."

"How long will that take?" Kayleesh shuffled backwards and brought her knees up to her chest, clasping them with her hands.

"Not long, but Hyganty and I would need to get to the system first without being attacked. We're in precisely the wrong place – both our quarters are on the other side of the bridge. We'd have to get through the swarm to access the system."

"I hope this doesn't sound offensive, but – do carnivorous dragonflies like the taste of your species – with you being -"

"They will eat anyone with two legs or more," Frarkk explained. "They're not insects. They're reptilian."

"Oh, so they're like actual dragons?"

"Actual dragons?"

"Never mind." Tom's stomach let him know that it was empty with a loud growl. *Radiakkan beer doesn't differ that much from Earth beer – I wonder if there is a kebab shop anywhere? That's if the dragonflies don't make supper of me first.* "So where is the system controlled from?"

"It's on the wall outside Nathan's room."

"What are you saying, Frarkk?" Kayleesh grabbed Tom's wrist and spoke into the timepiece. "Are you saying that *we* have to do this?"

"I'm afraid so," came the delayed response. "But we can talk you through it."

Kayleesh shrugged. "How hard can it be?"

Tom ducked as the door opened, half expecting a cloud of dragonflies to swoop in over their heads. But the only thing to come in unannounced was Nathan.

"We've got a job to do," Tom said and steered him back out into the passageway. "We've got to rid the ship of dragonflies."

"Dragonflies? How many people does it take to spray some bug spray?"

"They're not bugs," Tom explained, searching the walls for a device. "They're dragons."

"Dragons?" Nathan laughed. He seemed to still be intoxicated. "Do they breathe fire too?"

"I'm not sure I want to find out!"

"Is this the device?" Kayleesh stopped outside Nathan's door. There was a machine set flush with wall covered by a glass plate. Momentarily, Kayleesh's timepiece began to bleep.

"Are you near the defence system?" Frarkk asked.

"I think so," Kayleesh replied. She ran her hands around the edge of the glass. "How do I open it?"

"Push the glass at the right-hand edge and it will open." Kayleesh did so and the door swung open. "Now locate the keypad in the centre of the device and type in this code zero, three, eight, – arghh! Dragonflies! They've got into the –" Frarkk's voice broke off. Kayleesh spun round to face Tom, eyes wide.

"Oh no, now what do we do?"

"We should try and figure out the rest of the code," Nathan offered.

"But what about Hyganty and Frarkk? They're being attacked!"

"Exactly, so we should try to save them. It's no good us going down there and getting attacked too!"

"Frarkk!" Kayleesh hollered into her timepiece. "Hyganty! Can you hear me? What has happened?" By now, Kayleesh and Tom's timepieces were bleeping and flashing in unison, reacting to their racing heartbeats. "If we do manage to activate the system then maybe the others will get smoked out too."

"What a stupid system!" spat Tom.

"How could the dragonflies have got into their rooms?" wondered Nathan.

"If they can get into their rooms – then maybe they can get into this corridor too!" Screeched Kayleesh. "OK. Let's not panic. We can do this." She took a few deep breaths and her wrist soon ceased flashing and bleeping. Kayleesh calmly tapped in the first three numbers: zero, three, eight. There was room enough on the small screen for three more numbers. The device remained silent. Kayleesh tentatively typed in some random numbers; seven, four six. She pushed a key labelled submit. All three collectively held their breaths.

*Honk!* Came the negative audible response. The screen cleared itself. Kayleesh's shoulders fell.

"I expected little else," she admitted.

"Save yourselves!" Hyganty's voice emitted suddenly from Kayleesh's timepiece. "The entire swarm must be in the ship by now."

"You're all right!" Kayleesh gasped.

"We managed to swipe some away. We're hiding in the sanitation room in Frarkk's quarters."

"How did they get into your quarters?"

"They didn't – we ventured onto the bridge but... immediately regretted it."

"You what? OK, well can you give me the next three digits for the code?"

"Zero, Three, eight…"

"Zero, three, eight? You've already told us those ones. What comes next?"

"Zero…" Kayleesh's timepiece fell dead once more.

"What's happened?" Nathan asked. "Has it run out of power?"

"Impossible," Kayleesh shook her arm, staring at the communicator. "It charges as you move."

"Hyganty!" Tom called into his own timepiece. His cry was met with only static. "That's strange."

"I wish I had one of those devices. They seem great," Nathan joked. The sarcasm went over Kayleesh's head and landed flatly on the opposite wall.

"I've a feeling you'd get the same response," Kayleesh sighed. "OK, let's think about this. We need three more numbers. We don't know how many tries the system will allow before it locks up – *if* it locks up. And Hyganty and Frarkk are trapped together in a sanitation room in Frarkk's quarters at the other end of the ship."

"They seem to me like they might enjoy being trapped together, judging by the way they act around each other!" Nathan whispered to Tom.

"But then Hyganty did just say zero." Kayleesh continued. "Perhaps the next digit is zero, so it would be zero, three, eight, zero, something, something."

"The problem is the something, something," remarked Tom.

"Let me try a few combinations," Kayleesh offered.

"Then we'll venture out to find the others," said Nathan, boldly.

"We will, will we?" Tom gasped. "And just how are we going to get to them?"

Nathan shrugged. "All those rooms that we saw on the tour of the ship – one of them must store some kind of protective clothing."

"Good thinking." Tom's mouth spread into a smile.

The two Earthlings left Kayleesh with the device, which honked after each incorrect entry, and Kayleesh, cursing. They walked along the corridor in the direction which led further away from the bridge.

"What about this room? Didn't Hyganty say they stored space suits in here?" Nathan peered inside a room six doors down from his own. They went inside and were confronted with four large lockers. Tom pulled one of them open.
"Well remembered, Bud." Tom nodded. "However-" Tom said, reaching in and extending a suit out of the locker. "If we're going to wear these, we're going to have to grow considerably more appendages."

# CHAPTER 23

Jenrothrah Kale the Lymouse was sitting on the edge of his bunk with his head in his four hands. His huge dinner-plate ears were slumped onto his shoulders which were shaking with his abundant sobbing. Hannond Putt was sitting next to him, guiltily, subconsciously wriggling his toes.

"I'm so sorry," wailed the Lymouse. "The stench of my own gasses was enough to wake me up – it must be positively awful for you!"

"Not really. I can hardly smell it anymore. It really doesn't matter." Hannond said, truthfully. "You're sharing a cell with a Glorbian. We're not exactly famous for smelling of Rhorbian roses, ourselves." The Lymouse wailed all the more.

"But Lymice are renowned for being considerate and… and… oh my… *Guards!*" Jenrothrah stood up and called out. If the fourth wall of the cell hadn't consisted of Gorgon's eye rays, then he would surely have banged on it with his four pathetic fists. He had gotten himself in such a state, however, that Hannond wouldn't have been surprised if he had hurled himself at that deadly wall. "Guards! Let me out of here. I am not fit to be housed with another!"

A burly looking sentry One Seven Three appeared outside the cell. His eyes were slits through a face erupting with pustules. His voice was vociferous and authoritative.

"Get away from the wall, Lymouse! For the umpteenth time I will not put you in a cell of your own. Who do you think you are?"

"I'm a poor Lymouse. My cell mate doesn't deserve to be in my close company."

"I'm a poor Lymouse," One Seven Three mocked. "Pull yourself together and stop bothering the guards!"

"Yes, sir," Jenrothrah Kale whimpered pathetically. He sniffed and turned back to his bed.

Jenrothrah opened his mouth to speak.

"Please don't say you're sorry again," begged Hannond.

Drip twelve was making progress down the pane in the secret gambling room behind the laundry in sector thirteen. A thick drip of saliva fell from a Glorbian tongue and landed on the table between a pair of splayed out stubby hands. The perpetrator reigned in his tongue; his eyes still fixed on his wager.

*Come on little nanobots. Boost that drip to the bottom of the pane.*

Drip twelve accelerated past drip four, or was it drip five? It was difficult to keep an account of all of the drips in play. But Schlomm's eyes were focussed on his own drip. He wouldn't lose sight of it. But what was happening? Drip twelve was slowing down. It was *stopping*. This wasn't good. It was now travelling up the pane. Schlomm stood up, maddened.

"What is going on here?" But no one was listening to his protestations. They were too busy watching their own races and their own drips, whooping and booing. Schlomm looked about him for sentry Nine, in vain. He returned his gaze to the game pane once more – perhaps he had imagined it. But drip twelve was indisputably making its way back to the starting point. The game soon ended, to the sound of the joyous whooping of a Truxxian guard on the opposite side of the table. Schlomm scowled at the Truxxian momentarily then focussed his efforts on sentry One Five Six behind the counter. That damn Strellion! Why did I think I could trust him?

"You cheat!" Schlomm had barged his way to the front of the crowd. He banged both fists on the counter.

"Excuse me, sir?" The Strellion asked, as though margarine wouldn't melt in his oversized cheeks.

"You took my winnings and my spaceship! What did you do? Re-programme the nanobots?"

"Nanobots are illegal on this station, sentry One Four One. Surely you are aware of that?"

"Give me back my spaceship!" The Glorbian disguised as a guard demanded.

"You can have the chance to win your spaceship back. Would you like to play again?"

"No, I would not you big, thieving, dirty Strellion!"

"And racism is equally illegal. You're lucky I don't report you."

"And you're lucky I don't cut off your giant beak and make Strellion nose surprise with snot sauce!"

Tom Bowler was forcing a limb into the skinny trouser leg of the Submian spacesuit. The spacesuit was winning. Memories of his mum's once frequent skirmishes with his late Nan's surgical stockings came to mind. It used to take her up to an hour to ready her mother for a shopping trip. And Tom was puffing and panting like an old woman too. Nathan wasn't fairing much better. He was writhing around on the floor heaving at the garment, his laughter at the absurdity of the situation sapping most of his strength.

Two legs finally in and four spare trouser legs flapping about, Tom threaded his arms easily through the topmost holes, into the compartments reserved for the creature's giant pincers. The body was rather roomy with space enough for a broader body equipped with a set of wings. The helmets were ill-fitting but there was little that the humans could do. The pair turned to look at each other and collapsed in a succession of sniggers.

"Well if we don't manage to get through the swarm, then we might cause them to laugh their way into submission." Tom wiped away a tear. Tom and Nathan swish-swooshed their way back up the passageway; like two men in badly fitting shell suits who had been gorging on nitrous oxide.

Kayleesh's incorrect entries were still being met by the honk of denial.

"What are you two wearing?" Kayleesh laughed when she saw them. "Well anyway, I hope you have better luck than I'm having."

"Thanks Kayleesh – keep trying!" said Tom.

Between the two of them, they managed to remember the way to the bridge - although the hum of the swarm was a rather big clue. There was also an unnerving sound of the gnashing of teeth. Tom and Nathan looked at each other and gulped.

"If we crawl across the bridge, maybe they won't spot us," Nathan suggested. His poorly fitting helmet was entirely inappropriate for the mission, as was Tom's. There were more gaps and holes in them than in a block of mature Glorbian cheese. Tom's timepiece bleeped as he began to panic. He impulsively clapped his right hand over it to muffle the noise.

"But maybe they'll hear us! Useless, useless piece of technology." Tom dropped to the floor and began shuffling across the metallic floor on his stomach. He could hear the swarm overhead, buzzing and gnashing its thousands of tiny teeth. He dared not look up, wanting to keep his partially exposed face close to the ground. He had progressed several feet when suddenly, something grabbed his leg. Do these creatures have hands?

"We've got a bit of a problem, bud!" It was Nathan.

Tom found that the room was getting very warm.

"So they do breathe fire!" Tom gasped.

"Not exactly. If you open your eyes you'll see."

Tom tentatively opened his eyes and looked up at the swarming mass. They were surrounded by a team of creatures, hovering above them. The creatures were the size of large birds, but instead of wings they appeared to have an appendage on their backs which had the quality of a propeller which was keeping them afloat. Their bodies were covered in scales and each boasted two strong legs, their feet splayed out in front of them. At the end of each of these feet was a set of perilous looking claws - all of which were being pointed at the pair. Tom didn't know if it was the effect of shock, but he was convinced that the heat was being emitted from these claws. They were surrounded by a threatening dome of heat and noise. He began to sweat and felt nauseated. He wanted to be rid of his constrictive suit and escape. The sound of their tiny teeth and the humming propellers coupled with the heat was creating a stifling air of disorientation and confusion. Tom gasped in his discomfort and saw that Nathan was suffering too. Nathan started to cough. A wisp of smoke had drifted through a gap in his visor. Smoke?

"Tom, I think she's done it!" he hollered over the humming and gnashing. Tom nodded in agreement through coughs. The swarm was indeed starting to disperse.

"We should get out of here – if we hope to be able to breathe again." They stayed low, where the oxygen was more profuse. They crawled on across the bridge, down the passage and finally stepped out onto the access ramp. They watched, in awe, as the cluster of carnivorous dragon flies soon became a dot in the night sky.

"Zero, three, eight, zero, three, eight." Kayleesh had appeared at Tom's side.

"What?"

"That was the code. Hyganty wasn't repeating the first part of the code – he was saying the whole thing. He'd told us the entire code after all!"

"How did you figure that out?" asked Nathan.

"Trial and error," Kayleesh shrugged. "It's a pity I didn't realise sooner though."

"Yes, you would have saved us almost getting cooked alive by the little blighters!" Nathan blurted. "One question though – how does smoke scare away dragonflies? After all they breathe fire."

"No idea," Kayleesh thought for a moment. "That's aliens for you, I suppose. No offence."

"I don't think we've got rid of them for good," Frarkk said. He and Hyganty had joined them out on the ramp. Frarkk was holding a clutch of eggs with a number of his appendages. "I found these in my quarters. They evidently wanted to use the ship as a nest. It's doubtful that they'll abandon their young." Tom raised an eyebrow.

"What is it with this planet and eggs?"

Nathan was acting like an excitable infant. Eyes wide, his body weight jumping from one foot to the other like, he was grinning inanely at Tom.

"That was actually quite fun! We showed those monsters, didn't we? What's next?"

"You want some more excitement, do you?" Frarkk enquired.

"Oh yes. I have the taste for it now."

"In that case, you can take charge of these." He said calmly and emptied the clutch of dragonfly eggs into the excitable human's arms.

"Do I look like a hen?"

"A what?"

"It's a type of bird we have on Earth – a breed of fowl to be exact," Tom informed him in his best teacher voice.

"I didn't mean you to *hatch* the eggs." Frarkk shook his head. "Just transfer them to somewhere else so that the mother doesn't return to the ship."

"Oh, right. Do you fancy coming for a walk, Tom?"

Tom had wondered whether he could continue the conversation he was having with Kayleesh before the invading swarm had so rudely interrupted them. But she was yawning, and it seemed unlikely that she'd want to join him at this hour. That was the excuse he gave himself anyway. When in fact he had simply lost his nerve and had sobered up too much, thanks to the evening's events. Tom shrugged.

"Why not?"

"So what was Kayleesh doing in your room, bud?" Nathan nudged Tom when they were some way from the ship.

"I don't know what you mean," said Tom, but a coy smile betrayed his innocence.

"Come on... when I went into your quarters earlier she jumped down from your bunk. She was looking rather guilty."

"She was?" Tom's mouth creased at the edges. "I mean, er... we were just talking. She was telling me about her family."

"Right, of course she was, bud. You had a beautiful girl like Kayleesh in your room and you were talking about her family? Well unless you were asking her whether she has a sister for me then..."

"From what I've heard I don't think her sister would be your type," Tom laughed. He pictured Nathan with a much hairier version of the Augtopian he knew. "Kayleesh has, how shall I put it? Body image issues."

"Don't *all* girls?"

"Fair point."

"These eggs are getting a bit awkward to carry. How far do you think we need to take them?" Nathan was visibly struggling but refused to attempt to share the load with Tom for fear of breaking any. The journey was made all the more uncomfortable by the ill-fitting Submian suits the two of them were still sporting.

"There's a hedgerow a bit further on. Maybe we could set them down in a bush or something."

"Are you proposing that we build a nest?"

"Not if the dragonflies' idea of a nesting spot is a spaceship."

Nathan's arms were aching by the time that they reached the hedgerow. Two of the clutch did not complete the journey unbroken, but Nathan managed to set the remainder down safely.

Suddenly, a familiar sound alerted the two - a humming noise which was reaching a crescendo. They looked at each other, eyes wide.

"Run!" Tom yelled.

# CHAPTER 24

Schlomm Putt muttered to himself as he slip-slopped away from the laundry room on his two flat feet.

*Damn that Strellion! And damn me too! How could I have fallen for that? What have I achieved since I've been here? I haven't got any closer to rescuing Hannond. And now I've lost my only means off this molten rock. Hmm… it's time to step this mission up a few notches.*

He didn't know where he was heading, but Schlomm needed to get away from Sector Thirteen and away from the sentry wards. He was still lacking a digi-map. Of course, this was Schlomm Putt. And Schlomm Putt wouldn't be thinking of a *legitimate* way of acquiring one. That wouldn't be any fun. He'd had enough of gambling for one day, but perhaps there was another way of swindling a copy from one of the other guards.

He wondered for a moment whether Hannond had been missing him. Schlomm had to admit to himself that he was indeed missing his company. He hoped they weren't treating his brother too badly. He hadn't witnessed any poor behaviour of inmates yet, but one could never tell. It then occurred to him that he hadn't yet encountered *any* of Porriduum's inmates. It was then that he realised that he had, fortuitously, been walking in the right direction.

"To Gorgon Ray prisoner sectors." A sign boasted, next to which a door opened to reveal the interior of what Schlomm suspected was a transportation system. Schlomm grinned maliciously at the very idea of a Gorgon Ray cell wall. He was rather excited about the prospect of actually seeing beings incarcerated in this manner, even if one of them was his own brother.

It must have been a remarkable mind which conjured up such an ingenious idea. *I should like to shake Lord Mayrar by the tentacle some day and offer him my praise. And the architects too. Ingenious.*

Three sentry guards shuffled through the door and took seats on the tram. Schlomm took the opportunity and followed them in. One of the passengers spoke. He said simply,

"Sector four," and the door slid closed. The tram was spacious, with room for four ergonomic benches. Schlomm settled himself onto the bench opposite the other travellers and smiled to himself.

*Who needs a digi-map?*

"Leave us alone!" Nathan shouted at the sky as they ran. "We've just rescued your babies. Can't you show a little more gratitude?"

"It's… it's all right. It looks as though… they've… settled by the… nest. Phew! It is not easy to run wearing in these things." Tom panted as they finally came to a stop. A cloud of the creatures was bobbing over the spot where Nathan had laid down the eggs. "I don't think they'll bother us again."

"I hope they don't notice that they are missing two," said Nathan.

"Well there's not much we can do about that."

Tom wasn't sure how long he had slept, but both suns were shining brightly as he stood, stretching and yawning, on the ramp of the Submian ship; the furthest point that the ALSID field could reach. Hyganty had woken him from a deep slumber and presented him with a plate of sandwiches. It was almost like being back at home.

*Sandwiches for breakfast? At least they're not egg sandwiches. I've had enough of anything egg-shaped for a while.*

He had showered and shaved and thought about the previous day's dealings as he did so. It had been an eventful day. He had gone undercover as an employee in a Parliamentary Building; met a rather attractive female alien who had then proceeded to lay an egg; discovered that Raphyl's parents were in the very grounds of the building locked in time and then been thrown out of a public house because his Earth friend's rudeness. He had spent some quality time alone with Kayleesh for the first time in ages; and he and his fellow Earthling friend had ran around in Submian spacesuits, trying to escape from the swarm of carnivorous dragonflies; and then there had been more eggs. He admitted that there were things about Radiakka that he liked. Apart from the vicious wildlife and nationalistic natives it was a beautiful planet and, unlike Truxxe, had day and night. Long, beautiful days. He would have liked to have spent the day relaxing in the sun or exploring, but he knew that Raphyl still needed them to persist with the mission.

Tom was enjoying the warmth of the morning and chewing on his last sandwich, wondering what the new day had in store for him, when Nathan appeared looking rather sheepish.

"What is it, bud?" he asked him.

"You know we said that the dragonflies would be missing two eggs?"

"Er… yes I remember."

"Well… I think they may actually be missing three."

"What do you… oh."

The head of a creature with a long caterpillar-like body crawled up onto his friend's shoulder. On closer inspection, Tom decided that in fact it looked more like a fuzzy green ferret. Tom dropped the remainder of his sandwich in disbelief.

"What is *that?*"

"I think one of the eggs must have fallen through a gap in that stupid suit. When I woke up, I heard a cracking sound and then I found this thing, sitting on the floor and looking up at me. I can't seem to get rid of it!" Tom was laughing so hard that his eyes were watering. "It's not funny, Tom! I went to have a shower and when I got back it was sitting outside the door like a dog, squeaking at me."

"It was *pining* for you? That is priceless."

"I was going to step on it, but I just couldn't do it for some reason."

"You big softy. Well, I don't suppose it won't try and eat you if it thinks you're its mum!"

Nathan thumped him in the arm.

"I'm not its mum! I just didn't know what else to do with the thing."

"So you brought it outside for walkies?" Tom teased. "It's a strange thing. It must be at its larva stage or something." He prodded at it with a forefinger. The creature instantly recoiled and bristled into a green ball.

"Oi!" Nathan snapped.

"Oh, I'm sorry. I didn't mean to hurt your precious baby!"

"What's that?" Kayleesh asked, joining them.

"It's Nathan's new baby."

"Nathan's what?"

"Don't listen to him, Kayleesh. It hatched from one of those dragonfly eggs which must have fallen into the Submian suit I was wearing."

"It's not like you to torment people, Tom," admonished Kayleesh.

"No, I'm sorry. Blame Nathan – he brings out the juvenile side of me."

"Right." Kayleesh raised an eyebrow. "The egg seems to have hatched rather quickly. Are you sure it was one of the ones laid by that swarm yesterday?"

"It must be. Unless it was laid by Frarkk or Hyganty!" He and Tom chuckled.

"What are you going to do with it? It *is* quite cute."

"Er… well… would you like it?" Nathan held the creature out in his hands.

"Me?" Kayleesh appeared to be rather flattered by the gesture. "Well – I suppose I could look after it." Was Tom still dreaming? Was wise, sensible Kayleesh accepting such a gift from his reckless friend? It was a potentially dangerous gift at that. However, the fuzzy creature slithered its way back up Nathan's right arm and back to its perch on his shoulder. "Never mind. He seems to like you Nathan." She giggled.

"I guess you've chosen me, little fella," Nathan cooed, stroking it with the back of his hand. Tom rolled his eyes.

"Are you working undercover again today?" Kayleesh asked Tom.

"Apparently so." A bubble of excitement bumped into a bubble of anxiety in the pit of his stomach and produced a confusing fizz of emotion. "Well I need to find a way to get us underneath the statues, don't I?"

"What's he doing?" Nathan yelped. For the creature had descended his new friend and had proceeded to make light of a small pile of stones near the ramp. "He's eating rocks!"

"Strange creature," Kayleesh remarked. The Submians joined their passengers outside the ship. Hyganty eyed Nathan's new pet.

"I appreciate that you all worked together to save us from those beasts yesterday – but I don't think you should be holding on to one of their larvae."

"Do you think that they might come back for it?" asked Kayleesh.

"It's not that. Those creatures are very dangerous."

"They were pretty scary when they were in a swarm, but surely one small baby can't do much harm," Nathan protested.

"Well just be careful," Hyganty warned. "Are you ready for your second day at work, Tom?"

"I think so, but I'm not sure what I'm supposed to do. I'm not sure I can get away with not actually doing any work again."

"You'll think of something." Hyganty pressed the card containing Raghael and Mirrie's personalities into his hand. "Look after this."

"Come on, Tom," Nathan said. "How much work did you actually do when we went on work experience organised by the school?"

"Quite a lot actually – I worked on a busy news desk for two weeks. Slave labour that was!"

"OK, well that's just typical of you Tom, but I managed to spend most of my time at the factory just observing." Nathan stroked his new pet.

"You watched a bunch of machines wrap chocolate bars for a fortnight?"

"Oh no. I made the tea as well."

"Gracer!" Tom spotted a flame of burnt orange hair ahead of him in the red-lit corridor. Gracer Menille turned round and gave him a welcome smile.

"Hello Tom. What fun are we going to have today?"

"Fun? Yesterday you… you… er…"

"I what? Oh yes I laid the egg. I'd almost forgotten about that. It's not a big deal for my species. I'm sure I'll lay another before the day is out."

"Right-" Tom did not quite know what to say.

"By the way Tom, I managed to find something out about secret passageways. I knew you were interested in finding some so I did a bit of research."

"You did?" Tom gasped in delight. "How did you get the information?"

"Oh, I suspected that one or two people here might know more than they should. I used my feminine charms, fluttered my gills and there you have it – now I know more than I should!" she demonstrated a pulsing of her gills and a flutter of her lashes.

"I'm impressed," grinned Tom. "So where do we go?"

"Meet me in the red zone ladies sanitation room as the building closes to the public for the day," she winked.

There was an offer he could not refuse.

# CHAPTER 25

The tram passed door after identical door on its silent journey, and eventually came to a halt. Schlomm Putt stopped grinning when he realised that he had forgotten where to find his brother.

*Which sector did that amply-appendaged freak say he was on? Is he a class two prisoner in sector four or a class four prisoner in sector two? Which was it?*

The door by which they had stopped pinged open.

"Sector four," a disembodied voice announced.

The sentry who had requested the stop alighted.

I may as well try here first, thought Schlomm. He followed the passenger, a stern looking creature who carried his entire bodyweight on four muscular arms: Sentry Eighty-Five. Schlomm gulped as the higher-ranking guard turned to him.

"Don't forget your breathing apparatus, One Four One."

"Breathing apparatus?"

"You're in sector four – you're about to enter a different atmosphere."

"I am?" he gulped again. The Truxxian raised his monobrow.

"I mean, *I am*. Yes," he coughed and said gruffly. "Thank you for reminding me." *I'm in the wrong sector,* Schlomm panicked. *Hannond is an oxygen breather. At least, he was last time I saw him. Well I can't turn back now – that would look most suspicious. I'll have to pry around here for a while.*

Sentry Eighty-Five lifted a set of breathing apparatus from a clasp on the wall and proceeded to attach it in a manner which suggested he had done so a thousand times before. Schlomm took his time, pretending to busy himself with his timepiece, in hope that the guard would continue without him. The guard strode swiftly off down the corridor in the direction of the airlock. Now, which one should Schlomm choose? There was an array of different sized and shaped helmets bedecked with various lengths of tubing which left Schlomm scratching his head in bewilderment. He reached for one of the wider ones which resulted in being much too large for even Schlomm's globular Glorbian head. Another was fitted with so many tubes and funnels he didn't know where to put them all. He finally decided on a goldfish-bowl type affair which fitted rather snugly. A pipe ran from the bowl into the other half of the apparatus; a pack which he hoisted onto his back. After scrambling around in a circle for several moments, he eventually located the on switch.

He waited inside the airlock, watching from the safety of the helmet, as his vision was slowly marred by a wispy green ambience. The air was murky and dank as he stepped out of the airlock and into the cell block. His eyes soon adjusted and Schlomm could make out a long corridor stretching out in front of him. Serendipitously, the thick, green atmosphere served to highlight the Gorgon ray walls of the cells which lined the corridor. Schlomm grinned, his breath heavy and loud inside the helmet. He peered into the nearest cell. Two creatures lay snoring on their bunks, respiring easily in the foggy air. Schlomm could not identify their species. In the next cell another being was pacing up and down, muttering and growling. Schlomm imagined that was would be how he would react to being incarcerated too. He noticed that the prisoner was pacing dangerously close to the lethal cell wall. Schlomm slowed his pace, secretly hoping that the wall would be breached by a stray limb. He craved the opportunity to see the consequence of such an infringement. He had dreamed of it. But Schlomm was disappointed in this instance. The creature instead turned to him and glared.

"What are you staring at, O2 breather?"

"I think you'll find that I'm a sentry. Sentry One Four One, no less. I suggest that you respect that and keep that tongue still!"

"What tongue?" The prisoner opened his mouth to demonstrate this absence of a tongue and exposed three mean-looking sets of teeth.

"You don't scare me, prisoner. Not from behind that wall," Schlomm goaded. Maybe he'd make a lunge for him and there would be fried beast for supper.

"You don't scare me from behind this wall either," he growled. "I've been here far too long to fall for any of the tricks you dribblers pull."

"How long exactly?"

"Well, when I was first thrown in here, I only had the two sets of teeth."

"Right," Schlomm nodded slowly. "And in that time have you ever mixed with any of the prisoners on the other sectors by any chance?"

"Are you trying to trick me again, sentry? Hmm… I don't recognise you. You must be new. Or new to this sector, at least."

"You could say that. I'll leave you to your… pacing."

"No need to hurry off – I currently have a slot in my diary," he quipped. "You're not like the other guards. You have the shifty disposition of my previous cell mate, Clyoose - those same beady eyes."

"And what happened to him?"

"Oh, he got out. But not in the preferred way."

"Then which way?"

The prisoner remained silent. Schlomm nodded, understanding. He probed no further.

"So, what exactly are you up to?"

"Me? I'm not up to anything."

"That's how Clyoose used to say it. *Spit it out,* sentry! That's if you *are* indeed a sentry." Schlomm's brain was telling him to keep on walking – to leave sector four. He didn't owe this prisoner an explanation – surely conversing with him would only serve to scupper his plans. But then he didn't really *have* a plan and the prisoner couldn't do anything from behind that wall. Schlomm's feet remained staid. He gave in to his feet - for they were considerably larger than his brain. "Perhaps I can help you," the prisoner said. "As I told you – I'm not exactly overwhelmed with forthcoming engagements at the moment."

"Am I right in thinking that you might be missing the company of your old cell mate?" Schlomm went to scratch his chin in a ponderous manner, but the glass bowl got in the way. "It seems unusual behaviour for a convict to -"

"Don't be under the impression that I make a habit of befriending guards like a grassing little dribbler!" he spat. "If I thought you were actually a real sentry then I would sooner converse with a bowl of four-day old porridge!"

"Of course not. I apologise," Schlomm cowered. "But please keep your voice down – I don't want the whole cell block to know."

"So I was right?" He grinned, bearing all three sets of teeth. "Oh don't worry – the rest of the prisoners on this sector don't have a brain cell to share amongst them. So – what is your business here?"

"I'm here for my brother," Schlomm whispered gruffly.

"You are? I'm impressed! So your brother, he –"

"I am not going to spell it out to you – I thought that you implied you had a brain in there?"

The convict scowled. Then he laughed. "You really do remind me of my old cell mate. My name is Maal. I would shake you by the hand, but I don't want to lose mine."

"Schlomm Putt."

"Putt, you say? That name… I'm sure… no, maybe I am mistaken."

"Do you know something about my brother Hannond?"

"Hannond, you say?" Maal took to his pacing again. Schlomm tried to keep his voice low, but he was growing fervent.

"If you know something, you need to tell me!" he demanded.

"*Do* I now? And what would this gem of information be worth?" Maal ceased his pacing. Schlomm sighed.

"I will ensure that you are paid handsomely if you could tell me as much as you know."

Tom Bowler did as Nathan had suggested and observed the goings on of the Parliamentary Building that day, playing the part of an interested potential future employee. He pretended to help marshal groups of visitors as they toured the huge edifice and kept out of the way of anyone who looked as though they were of high official status. He did not catch sight of Gracer in his time-biding hours, even at lunchtime, but trusted that she would adhere to their planned meeting.

When it was finally time, Tom followed signs to the red zone ladies sanitation room – deciding that this option would be safer than asking someone for directions. He found it with some ease and, ensuring that no one was around him, slipped into the floral-fragranced room. The tiles underfoot were wet as though they had been recently cleaned. Where was Gracer?

*What am I doing?*

The door opened.

"I'm glad you found it OK," came Gracer's deep tones, flooding the gent in the ladies' room with relief.

"So am I. But I'd rather not spend too long in here if I can help it. Where is the-"

"Quiet!" Gracer put a hand to his mouth. "Someone's coming."

Tom unthinkingly burst into one of the cubicles. It was occupied.

A scream. A loud scream from a yellow being.

"Get out! Get Out!"

Tom screamed too, in surprise, and ran back out of the cubicle. His foot slipped on the tiles and his face met with the wet floor. A pair of blue feet and a trio of yellow feet appeared beside him as he struggled to stand, his legs skidding in all directions. Tom realised he was the worst undercover agent in existence. What was he doing, writhing around on the floor in a lady's bathroom, drawing all this attention to himself?

"Tom, what are you doing? Come on." Gracer beckoned him from a cubicle at the far end of the bathroom. He crawled across the sopping floor with all the dignity of an incontinent chimpanzee. Finally, Gracer closed the door behind him. Tom scanned his eyes around the small space, feeling around the floor underneath the toilet. "Again, I ask you Tom – what are you doing?"

"Looking for the exit – where is the doorway to the passage?"

"Well it's not in here," Gracer guffawed.

"What do you mean? Well, why on – Radiakka – did you drag me in here?"

"I thought it would be a discreet meeting point," she said simply.

*"Discreet?* Maybe for you but – oh never mind. So where do we go from here?"

"Follow me." Gracer led the mortified human past a gathering of aghast females and back out into the red zone corridor.

They soon came to a room marked Personnel Dept. She unlocked the door and gestured for him to follow.

"How did you manage to get a key?"

"This is my office," she said casually.

"*You work in personnel?* So, you know…"

"…I know that your name isn't actually registered for work experience here, yes," she finished. "But I like you, Tom. I've not met anyone like you so I'm giving you a free pass – so to speak." Tom simply grinned. "Come on, the entrance to the passageway is underneath my desk, over here." Tom's feet stopped and his eyeballs bulged.

"You had a trapdoor to a secret passageway under your desk all this time and you never knew until now?"

"I never needed to know," Gracer shrugged. "Not until I met you, now come on."

The passageway was as long and cramped as Tom had expected it to be. His brain was buzzing with excited neurons. He clutched the card in his hand, longing to reunite its contents with its original owners. Gracer was ahead of him, her torchlight guiding their way as she half hummed, half whistled an unrecognisable tune. The tune in Tom's head was the one made famous by the film The Great Escape. He chuckled to himself.

"What are you planning on doing when you get to the end of this passageway, anyway?" she called.

"You'll see. If it works, then it will be pretty amazing! You won't tell anyone about this little adventure will you?"

"And get myself into trouble? No fear!" Suddenly, Gracer's torchlight flickered off, rendering them in complete blackness.

"Oh no!" Tom ground to a halt.

"It's a pity about the torch," Gracer said in matter-of-fact tones. "You can still see a little though, can't you?"

"What? No, of course not, there's no light to see by!"

"Your species is certainly very strange. Here." Tom felt Gracer grasp him by the arm. "I'll guide you. I can make out some of the tunnel. We'll have to watch our step though." The neurons in Tom's brain buzzed around a little faster in the close proximity of the tall girl. He could see nothing but was comforted by the sweet scent which radiated from her, coupled with her odd whistle hum. They stumbled once or twice on the uneven ground until a short while later his guide stopped. As did her whistle hum.

"I think we're here. Or somewhere, at least. We've reached the end of this passageway anyway. A slightly narrower tunnel veers off down and to the right, but it looks as though we've arrived at some kind of chamber," her voice echoed slightly in the rocky grotto. "There's something in the centre. I will need a closer look to make out any detail." Gracer abandoned his side and he heard her footsteps on the hard ground as she moved away from him. "It looks like the base of some kind of construction."

"I think I can make it out too," Tom said. "There must be some light coming in from above." He walked towards the construction base, his eyes adjusting to the dim light. "It looks like it could be the base of one of the statues – we found them, Gracer!" He felt around the rocky surface of the one nearest to him. Would he be successful this time? Sure enough, his hands met with the cold smoothness of technology; he had found the card drive. He held the card up to the slot.

He gulped. "Here goes!"

Tom Bowler and Gracer Menille shielded their eyes as their retinas were violated by bright, sharp light. The light was accompanied by a loud grinding sound: rock on rock. The ground shook slightly, and they held on to each other for safety. The brightness subsided and the two of them were confronted by the very statues of Mirrie and Raghael; they had descended into the chamber. Only they were no longer statues. Mirrie's left hand was twitching. Her husband was cricking his neck as though he was merely awakening from a Sunday evening snooze. Tom gasped. Hyganty had been right – Raphyl's parents were still alive.

"Tom, what is going on?" Gracer mouthed. Tom grinned at her as her spoke into his timepiece.

"Raghael and Mirrie are awake."

# CHAPTER 26

Two confused Truxxians, two smug Submians, Kayleesh, Nathan, Gracer and an especially smug Earthling were sitting in a rather comfortable room aboard the Submian spaceship. The two Truxxians became less confused, however, as their predicament was explained to them. Gracer beamed as the reasons for her and Tom's adventure underneath the Parliamentary Building grounds unfurled.

"Are you two really Raphyl's parents?" Nathan asked.

"Of course. Haven't you been listening?" Kayleesh admonished him. Nathan ignored her.

"You were asleep for over three hundred years?"

"Apparently so," Raghael shrugged. "But the real issue here is that we have to rescue our son."

"Hold on," said Frarkk. "Before we get to that we need to know what happened. Raphyl obviously didn't perform patricide – or matricide for that matter – so why was he accused? And why were the two of you frozen all this time?"

"How could they know what happened when they were asleep?" asked Tom.

"I suspect it all has something to do with Truxxian/Radiakkan relations," Mirrie sighed. "Or lack of them. We were Truxxian born and as celebrities of our time, in the architectural circles at least, Truxxe was proud of this fact." Her voice was soft and her tone, modest. Tom could detect some of Raphyl's mannerisms in her movements, which served to amuse him. Mirrie brushed a lock of her long, violet hair behind an ear. "But when we created ACD, we took a lot of the funding from this rich land and as our fame grew we were commissioned to build the Wheyland Parliamentary Building. We thought that this would be the perfect opportunity to help pay back some of our initial loan."

"Even after the success of our design for the construction on the prison planet, we were still indebted to Radiakkan banks," Raghael added, solemnly. "They are a harsh people – particularly towards off-worlders."

"And yet they celebrated you in the grounds of this country's most significant building?" Tom asked. "You'd have thought that they would only have statues of Radiakkans if they're as prejudiced as they seem to be."

"It is unusual, yes," Mirrie replied. "I don't think they would have admitted that we were the designers of their most distinguished building if we hadn't had won the Galactic Architectural Award. Once they discovered ACD had achieved this accomplishment they wanted to claim us as theirs – they had helped to fund the company after all."

"But it doesn't explain why they put you in suspended animation like that – and then framed your son!" Kayleesh wondered.

"My memory is vague," Raghael put four long fingers to his balding cranium. "But I believe that the Radiakkans wanted to keep us for themselves – as immortal trophies. We weren't strong enough to resist and Raphyl evidently escaped onto one of the other freezing podiums before they could stop him. The Radiakkans clearly abandoned his cryo podium and simply brought both of ours back to their planet."

"So why didn't the Truxxian police wake Raphyl when they found that you were both gone and that he had frozen himself?" Tom asked.

"We weren't there so it is impossible to know for certain," Mirrie replied. A look of concern flashed across her face. "But if he had climbed onto a podium without using a personality disc to protect his mind while he was frozen then it would have been too risky to thaw him before the set time elapsed."

"And yet he set the time to three hundred years and survived," pondered Tom.

"As I have mentioned before," Hyganty piped up, "it is likely that Raphyl took action in a panic – perhaps he thought three hundred years to be sufficient. It was a risk that he didn't use the safety drive." He addressed the Truxxians. "Mr. and Mrs… I mean Raghael and Mirrie, when you next see your son he may not be as you remember him. Last time we saw him he was happy and well but…"

"What Hyganty is trying to say," Kayleesh interjected, "is that Raphyl is now a dim-witted, indolent little-"

"Kayleesh!" Tom reprimanded.

"You didn't let me finish!" Kayleesh scowled. "But we do love him very much and would really like to help you return him to Truxxe!" Her scowl had morphed into a margarine-wouldn't-melt smile.

"Indeed," Raghael raised his shaggy monobrow. "So, you want our testimony to prove that he didn't murder us?"

"That's simple – our being alive is proof enough," Mirrie chuckled. Tom felt reassured. The atmosphere was rather a homely one. He was spurred on by the thought that soon Raphyl would be back in their midst and that his friend would be reunited with his parents once more.

"We shouldn't linger on this planet much longer," Frarkk warned. "Once dawn breaks and the absence of the statues is apparent they will start looking for us."

"If you're worried that I will say anything to my employers then you needn't be," Gracer said sincerely. "If I need to contact you all, I will. On which area of Truxxe can I find you?"

Nathan, Tom and Kayleesh were discussing the recent events in Tom's quarters on the Submian ship later that evening. Nathan seemed to be more interested in his new pet, however. He had gathered a handful of stones and was rolling them across the floor in a bid to interact with the creature. It shuffled along, quite dutifully, munching on each morsel.

"I wonder what I should call him," he pondered. Sideways glances jabbed at him from both Tom and Kayleesh, who continued with their conversation. Suddenly, Hyganty burst into the room, startling everyone. Not least the creature, which had been nibbling at a particularly large stone and impulsively withdrew into a ball.

. "I've just been reading up on the local wildlife," Hyganty uttered. "Those dragonflies are no ordinary creatures."

"Yes, they are quite odd – how do they produce so much heat and why on Earth – I mean Radiakka – are they called dragonflies?" mused Nathan.

"Well perhaps it's because they fly and they produce heat like the mythical creatures," Kayleesh shrugged.

"So you do know about dragons?" Tom said, mostly to himself.

"Please – all of you!" Hyganty knelt, as far away from the creature as he could manage without being in the next room and explained. "These creatures are part of ancient mythology if that's what you mean. Dragons don't actually exist of course. They are scientifically impossible; or at least very improbable. These creatures produce heat by digesting radioactive ores and the energy is concentrated in their extremities. Their claws are their main weapon, not their teeth."

"So they're not carnivorous? Well that's all right then. They're just a little feisty," Nathan beamed, placing down the remainder of the pebbles and scooping up the animal in his hands.

"No, I discovered that they're not indeed carnivorous… truth is much worse than I feared. They're radioactive."

"What?" Nathan dropped the creature as though it had administered an electric shock. It gave a little squeal of alarm but seemed unharmed. It shuffled away and began devouring the stone pile.

"So unfortunately, we'll all have a degree of radiation poisoning from being exposed to the dragon flies."

*Unfortunately?* thought Tom. *Is radiation poisoning classed merely a mild annoyance for him?*

"Well that explains why he's so fond of these rocks," said Nathan.

"Quite. We need to find treatment for radiation poisoning. Before it's too late."

In light of the urgency of the situation, the wait until dawn had been aborted. The ship's passengers quickly strapped themselves into flight chairs and the crew members stationed themselves on the bridge, ready for take-off.

*More delays in rescuing Raphyl,* though Tom.

"Where do you think they're taking us?" Nathan asked.

"Nathan – you really should brace yourself for the take off!" Tom alerted him. "It won't be a smooth one."

After the craft's typically traumatic take-off, Raphyl's parents spoke of their work as architects. They spoke not boastfully but answered all questions the three friends put to them with enthusiasm.

"During my short time at the Parliamentary Building I was stunned by the sophistication of the design," said Tom. "It seemed to be full of complex routes and of course – secret passageways. I can't believe that anyone working there would know the layout of the entire place."

"You could say that the style is a hallmark of ours," Mirrie smiled. She and Raghael exchanged knowing looks. "I don't believe that anyone apart from the two of us knows the entire blueprint of the Porriduum prison – even three-hundred years on. That was the beauty of contracting out to so many builders. In fact, I shall tell you a secret about our prison design."

"Mirrie – do you think that you should?" Raghael shot her a warning glance.

"Oh, what do we have to lose, Raghael?" she shrugged, and, at the cue of her partner's softening expression, she continued. "Authority Construction Designs – *that is, Raghael and I* – designed a fail-safe in the prison plans. You see, at that time, we were nervous of the stringent, fickle laws which are passed in the very building we designed on Radiakka. We were aware that our mounting debts to Radiakka did not bear favourably with them. We pre-supposed that should either of us ever be unfortunate enough to be exiled to the dreadful place that we would at least have a chance. So that if we were trapped in that damned structure we would have had a fighting chance to escape alive."

Three jaws raced to be the first to hit the floor as Tom, Nathan and Kayleesh gasped.

"Are you telling us that you two engineered a way out of Porriduum?" Kayleesh said, before either of the other two could find the right words. "That is impressive. How clever!" But Raghael's sorrowful words contrasted with Kayleesh's elated utterings.

"We are the only ones who know the entire structure of the place," Raghael lowered his head and sighed. "If only we had passed the information onto our son. We could have saved him weeks of unnecessary imprisonment. I'm just grateful that you reanimated us so that we can rescue him now."

# CHAPTER 27

Maal bared his three sets of teeth at Schlomm Putt in a kind of twisted grin. Schlomm keenly wanted the information that this creature held behind those knowing eyes. That was if he was being sincere – perhaps he was toying with him. He had been tricked already on this planet by undesirables and once was enough for Schlomm. After all, it was he who was supposed to be the devious one. It had always been him, and yet he had been stung by the Strellion kind again. The situation needed rectifying. He needed to find his brother and escape with him so that they could re-form their troublesome duo and wreak havoc on the galaxy for some ill-gotten gains; like they used to.

Perhaps he was getting too old for all this now. Perhaps their pilfering, plotting days were over. Schlomm shook the thought from his head – he refused to believe it. No, he would rescue Hannond and the two of them would plot together once more.

"Name your price," he said, finally.

"Five crates of the finest Glorbian whiskey."

"Would they allow the consumption of it in here?"

"No. But my sentence will be complete in seven Porriduum weeks and I should like the opportunity to celebrating in style."

"Very well – I shall arrange a delivery to your home once I get off this stinking rock – if I ever get off it."

"Then I shall keep my part of the bargain," Maal said. "Hannond has been incarcerated with the most pathetic creature in the galaxy – a Lymouse by the name of Jenrothrah Kale."

"He can't be any more pathetic than Hannond," Schlomm snorted.

"You've obviously never encountered a Lymouse. If your brother wasn't insane when he arrived, then he will be by the time he is released. Lymice are the most irritatingly polite, pitiable creatures you could ever stumble upon."

"Is this all you have to tell me? I don't think that scrap of information is worth even a bottle of Glorbian grog," he scowled. Maal took to his pacing once more.

"As I said, you have obviously never met a Lymouse. They have a particular quality about them. Lymice are disgustingly courteous creatures. They are courteous to the extreme – so much so that the fact that there is one sitting in a prison cell is significant – it never happens. They don't commit crimes – not generally - they're just too *nice.*" Maal looked as though he was trying to swallow a whole lemon. "Their revoltingly chivalrous nature extends to the point that they don't even break wind! Not just in public, but at all. Ever. At least - not in the conventional way." Maal gave a raucous cough and his tone mellowed by several notches. "They have evolved not to let loose in the way that we would. Their bodies have evolved to compensate. They say that the body of a Lymouse produces a high number of anaerobic bacteria in the colon because of a diet rich in Lacbeetle milk, to which they are notoriously intolerant. But the stupid Lymice are addicted to the taste and eat little else, which satisfies the bacteria which continues to grow and produce excess hydrogen. So, when the hydrogen exits the body with the rest of the flatus gasses, it is encased in a bubble which saves the Lymice from embarrassment as it rises out of their scruffy underpants and floats away; noiseless and odour controlled."

"You speak with some intelligence," Schlomm was taken aback. "You're not how you seem at first glance, are you?"

"All right, all right, I'm a scientist – but don't tell anyone." Maal leaned forward as far as the deadly divide would allow. "I only have a few more weeks to survive – I've kept the tough guy act up for this long. I don't want to risk losing face now!"

Schlomm grinned. He now had the advantage, should this being ever double-cross him. Maal continued.

"Porridge on Porriduum is not made from Lacbeetle milk, though, which is another reason why Lymice avoid being exiled here as far as possible. I have news that Jenrothrah, however, has recently received a special food parcel from the outside – a consignment of Lacbeetle milk, no less."

"So basically, he's currently farting away in his prison cell. Schlomm isn't in any real danger other than being gassed to death then, should one of those bubbles burst." Schlomm uttered, impatience getting the better of him.

"The bubbles have another quality – when exposed to a naked flame – kaboom!"

"Kaboom?"

"And that's if there's just one of them in the open air. If one was slotted into the shell of a Blandart beast for example – it would be *kaboom to the power of fifty!* For instead of exploding in all directions – the shell would focus the energy of the blast against whatever you should want to destroy – without the risk of inuring yourself. And there is some chance that the beast would emerge unscathed too."

"Blandart beasts – I've heard of those," Schlomm's beady eyes were twinkling. "They do have an indentation in their shell; they use it to carry their young. Vile creatures – never do business with a Blandart beast and worse still - never spill his pint. Are there any in this prison?" he speculated. Maal laughed.

"As many as there are dentists on my home world," Maal bared his many teeth. "Of course there are. They're Blandart beasts!"

"Good point," Schlomm felt foolish for having asked. "Maal – I think I may have a plan. I just want to know – how did you know that Lymice bubbles would create an explosion in the back of a Blandart beast?"

"I er… I was involved in a little experimentation in my old lab," he said, quietly.

"I see, and where did your discovery lead you?"

"Here," Maal sighed and looked about his cramped chamber.

"I see."

The hand-steps of Sentry Eighty-Five with whom Schlomm had shared the tram ride panicked him and he stepped away from the cell. He didn't want to be seen chatting with a prisoner by an already suspicious guard. He shot a disquieting look at Schlomm but continued on his way on his four limbs.

"Your information has indeed been of use," Schlomm whispered, once they were out of earshot. "I may call on you again and make use of your oddly scientific brain. In the meantime, I need to fuel my thoughts with a double cheeseburger."

When the passengers disembarked from the Submian craft, Tom realised that Hyganty and Frarkk had docked the ship back in the familiar TSS complex.

"What a strange place!" Mirrie remarked as they descended the ramp. "Where are we?" She was visibly marvelling at the grandiose docking bay, mouth agape.

"This is Truxxe… your home planet," Tom quavered.

"Really? This is… well… it has been a long three hundred years!"

"Are you impressed by this, Mirrie? Look what they've done to the place!" Raghael spat, in repugnance.

"Oh, I don't know – things have to move on, don't they?" She touched her partner's arm, lightly. "So, they found a way to resolve the poverty on the planet then?" she turned to Tom. He was saved from having to answer this awkward question by Hyganty's bossy tones.

"Come along all of you – the sooner we get to the Clinicarium on floor seventeen, the better." The six of them followed the authoritative insect across the docking bay like a class of children on a school trip. Tom was no stranger to the Clinicarium level but was in no rush to be first to arrive, radiation poisoning or no radiation poisoning.

*What if they don't realise I'm human again and they start hacking off my limbs?* He shuddered at the memory of his encounter with Medic Flonce.

Tom's wish to delay the procedure was quickly granted. A bony, grey hand appeared on his shoulder.

"Tom Bowler," a commanding voice spoke. Tom spun round. "I am arresting you on suspicion of unlawful copyright breach."

# CHAPTER 28

"That's ridiculous." Nathan squared up to the Gray. He recognised the small, stern creature as one of the ones which had 'abducted' him from his back garden. "Tom wouldn't do anything unlawful – not Tom Bowler." The Gray pushed the human out of the way with a bony hand and turned again to Tom.

"We have reason to believe that you have made copies of no less than twenty-five melodies, for your personal listening pleasure, without payment to the artists."

"Oh that," Tom's shoulders fell. "But I didn't hurt anyone – I didn't know it was illegal. I found the blank cards in-" Tom stopped himself from incriminating Raphyl any further, "-I found them."

"Ignorance of the law does not excuse you from the consequences," he stated. His black, almond-shaped eyes narrowed.

"Consequences?" said Tom. "If there is a fine, I will happily pay it now – I have some Ds." He proceeded to rummage in his pocket.

"There will be no fine,"

"Then we will be on our way," Hyganty declared.

"Regrettably, this young being will not be accompanying you," the Gray said bitterly. "He will be accompanying me." At first Tom thought that the lithe creature had disclosed a gun, as he swiftly touched a device to his lower arm before activating a mechanism at its base. A red band slithered out of the contraption and circumnavigated around his wrist before Tom had the chance to pull away. Tom recognised the device from when he and Kayleesh had been issued with green tags on the prison level. But this tag was red.

Cursing himself for being almost envious of Nathan when he had first seen the relative luxury of his cell, Tom realised that things did not seem so pleasant from the other side of the metal door. In a cruel twist of fate, he had even been confined in the same cell - 7A.

"Oh, sweet irony!" Tom called out to the creator of the law of sod. He was pacing around the chamber, fists clenching at tufts of hair, eyes full of tears. What had he done?

*Why did I copy those stupid songs? Didn't I have enough to keep me entertained, what with being on an alien planet and everything? It didn't even occur to me that I was doing anything illegal. I didn't even like the music all that much.* Tom hollered in the lonely cell, letting out his frustration at the futility of the situation. *I have spent the last few weeks trying to get friends out of prison cells and I end up in one myself. I think I'll just give up. Give up and go home. If only I could.*

Home. He'd never so much as been kept in detention at school. What was he doing in a prison cell? A tear rolled down his cheek as he flopped down onto the ergonomic bed. He rolled over and tried to punch the bed beneath him in anger, but the pliable material simply accommodated to each blow, which served only to anger him further. How was he going to rescue Raphyl now? Would Mirrie, Raghael and the others prove his innocence without him in their company? Would they leave him here – a mere after-thought? Perhaps he was being selfish – Tom knew that Raphyl's predicament on Porriduum was much worse than his own. At least he was still on Truxxe. But then he comprehended that at least Raphyl was innocent, just as Nathan had been innocent. Tom had been the only one of the three who had essentially committed a crime. The rage Tom felt bubbling inside him began to subside. The feeling was replaced with one of calm and submission. As expected, the pherobot guard clattered its way into the cell. He smiled – perhaps it had come to let in a group of visitors. How he longed to see Kayleesh, even though it had been a mere two hours since his arrival on the prison level. But alas, the only person who trailed behind the robot was the Gray who had arrested him. Tom shook his head, sadly.

"I've learned my lesson – I won't copy any more music. But I have to get off this level," he pleaded. "I have burgers to sell – people need their burgers. I could give you a free burger every day for the rest of my stay on the planetoid. And a milkshake – anything you –"

"- It is not one of our laws you have broken," the policeman barked. "But bribing a policeman *is,* so you'd better stop there, young human!"

"What? So I haven't broken one of your laws?" A butterfly of hope soared in his stomach.

"But the band who wrote one of the melodies you reproduced is not native to Truxxe. And they have chosen to press charges." The butterfly in Tom's stomach did a nose-dive. "They are the Radiakkan group Screamba."

Radiakkan? The butterfly keeled over and withered. What is it with that race?

"In case you need to be reminded to which melody I am referring; I have a card with me on this portable melody mech." He patted a compact version of his Truxxian hi-fi, which was clipped to his belt. "An original copy, may I add." Tom put his head in his hands as the machine clicked into life and the sound of the female vocalist wailing against electric strings, percussion and androgynous backing vocals filled the cell.

Tom no longer found the track amusing.

"Do you recognise this melody?"

"I… oh you know that I do," Tom sobbed. "So how long do I have to stay here? When will my sentence be over?"

"Oh, you won't have to stay here long." The policeman clicked off the device. "Only until the next available window."

"Next available window?" No, no, no. This can't be happening!

# CHAPTER 29

Two young friends, green tags around their wrists, tentatively followed the pherobot guard into cell 7A. Instead of the welcoming, perhaps anxious-looking features they knew so well, they were confronted with a face full of tears. The pherobot left and Kayleesh ran over to Tom and cradled his sobbing head in her arms.

"Don't cry, Tom. You'll get out of here – you said yourself that these cells are better furnished than our quarters!" She sat back on the bed and held his hand. This comforting act of kindness was nullified by the pain that Tom felt. The sheer horror. That word. That dreadful word.

"Porriduum," he managed.

"Yes, Raphyl will soon be released from Porriduum – and you'll be released from here and –"

"You don't understand. I'm being sent to Porriduum!"

"You're what?" Nathan crumpled to the floor and stared at Tom. Even Kayleesh didn't have anything optimistic to say in this instance. Kayleesh and Nathan both simply gawped at him. More tears.

"I-I-I'm just so useless." Tom shook his head. He was so frightened that he was shivering. Kayleesh instinctively drew him close to her, an arm round his shoulder, a hand still on his. "How do I get myself into these situations?" He explained that the Radiakkan band, Screamba, had pressed charges and that there was nothing that Truxxe's legal system could do. Radiakka was just too strong.

"Damned planet," Kayleesh growled. "I wish I'd never heard of it! Those detestable Radiakkans. How dare they do this to you?" She pulled him close into an embrace. Tom enjoyed the moment.

*This might be the last time I see any of them. This might be as far as Kayleesh and I go – a sympathy squeeze.* He pulled her close to him and gave her a soft kiss on her cheek, which he found was wet with her own tears. He was reminded that Nathan was still in the room when he spoke.

"You shouldn't really be worrying, Bud." He got to his feet.

"Why ever not?" Kayleesh admonished him. "I'd like to see you not worry if you were going to be banished to the prison planet!"

"I wouldn't be worrying," he said rather smugly. Kayleesh and Tom broke their embrace. Nathan's eyes twinkled. "Not if I knew someone who knew a way out of there – not if I knew Mirrie and Raghael."

"You genius!" Tom laughed. "Of course! They know the entire layout of the place – they know how I can escape!"

"I don't know, Tom," Kayleesh quavered. "Isn't it a bit risky? You'd be a fugitive if you escaped. Is it such a good idea?"

"Would you rather I festered away in there? Waiting for the Radiakkan law to change or my sentence to end? I doubt that either would be swift."

"You're right," she smiled at him, stroking his hand fondly. "And if you do manage to escape, you'd be a celebrity – no one has ever achieved it before. Well, maybe anyway. I don't... like... to think about the alternative."

"Well let's not think that far ahead just yet," Nathan said. "Our priority is to get that important information from the brains of those clever little Truxxians into yours. I'll inform Raghael and Mirrie."

Schlomm Putt finally reached sector four. He had made a detour to the staff canteen, however, where he had rested for longer than he had intended as he was caught up in the occupation of observing an unusually attractive female sentry polish her fingernails. He had been fascinated by the fact that her fingernails were on her head and that she required the use of an arrangement of mirrors in order to be able to go about the task.

But now he was on the correct sector, breathing without the aid of complicated apparatus and was able to see the cells clearly for the first time; on account of them not being obscured by a green haze. He gave a fresh smirk of admiration as he walked the corridor, marvelling at the sheer brilliance of the design. A familiar body came into view in one of the cells which lined the corridor. Either his brother had not been permitted to wash since being incarcerated, or he had acquired a rather deep tan during his visit to Radiakka.

"Schlomm!" Hannond leaped off his bunk and greeted him, nudging Jenrothrah Kale out of the way as he neared the fatal partition.

"Oh, do excuse me," whined the Lymouse. "Please accept my deepest apologies that my clumsy frame was in your path." Jenrothrah shook his large ears in dismay and skulked away to his bunk. Schlomm shook his own head in dismay at the actions of the dismal creature.

"Maal wasn't wrong about Lymice," he muttered.

"Who?" Hannond asked. "Anyway, what are you doing here, Schlomm? How?"

"Before I explain how I got in, I'm going to explain how I'm going to get us out." Schlomm looked over his brother's rounded shoulder at his simpering cellmate. He whispered, "Unfortunately, we're going to need the help of your pathetic little friend over there. Well, part of him anyway."

The lilac faces of the customarily surname-less Truxxians, Raghael and Mirrie, were beacons of hope for Tom the following morning. He hadn't been permitted any further guests on the same day as his visit from Kayleesh and Nathan and the hours between the two visits had been painfully long for the caged human. He had barely slept.

Raphyl's mother was sitting on the cell's only ergonomic chair and his father had taken to pacing up and down in deep thought. The look of trepidation on the female's face was reminiscent of the expression on Tom's mother's face when she had been troubled by the belief that her son was involved in drugs. The cause of Tom's strange behaviour, unbeknown to his mother however, had in fact been due to the fact that he had been contemplating the insane prospect of moving away from the Milky Way.

"As far as I can see, there is no decision to be made, Raghael," said Mirrie. She added in a whisper, "The welfare of our son is at stake here. We need to tell the boy our clandestine escape route. We can trust him."

I *am* in the room, thought Tom. But said nothing.

"I am aware of the situation, Mirrie. And I believe we can trust him, but it's not that simple is it? It's not as though there is a magical button that can be pressed, and he will simply be teleported back home."

"I know," Mirrie sighed.

"So how complicated is this secret escape?" Tom asked.

"Probably too complicated for you to remember all of it. There's just too much for you to consider – it's not straight forward."

"But I rescued the two of you from the labyrinthine Wheyland Parliamentary Building," Tom protested. He omitted the minor detail of Gracer Menille being his personal tour guide. "And I am good at retaining information. I was the top of my class at school – I passed every exam I took with good grades."

"These words are all irrelevant, Tom," Raghael barked. Then is voice softened. "I'm just afraid that you don't realise quite what you're risking. If this plan isn't followed exactly-"

"It will be," Tom stood up and looked Raghael in the eye.

"- If this plan is not followed exactly," Raghael reiterated, "then the consequences for you will be even harsher. You will be downgraded from the status of a condemned petty thief to that of a failed escapee – they will not be sympathetic towards you!"

"I realise that, but it's worth the risk. I can do this." The words came out of Tom's mouth before he could catch them and thrust them back into his lungs. This was a step too far, surely? Even for his new adventurous self. What was he thinking?

"I have faith in you, Tom," Mirrie smiled at him.

Tom Bowler studied the detailed drawing Raghael had fashioned for him. It contained more lines than the complete works of Shakespeare and more arrows than a Middle Earth battle. How was he going to memorise all these routes and directions? If only he could take personal possessions on board. He would be like an actor treading the boards first time without his script. Only there would be no prompt. He had to memorise every detail of the plan.

He was seriously beginning to doubt his ability to follow through with such a complicated, precise expedition. Part of him wished that Kayleesh was coming to the dreadful place with him – her brain was adept at formulating plans and seeing things from all angles. He turned the page this way and that, muttering the instructions to himself. It was like trying to memorise a complex computer game walkthrough and only having one life in which to complete it. Raghael had informed Tom that prisoners of his class were stationed on sector two and that there was a possibility that Raphyl wouldn't be too far away; particularly as they were both oxygen breathers. These words did little to comfort Tom as he knew that part of his passage to freedom would entail journeying through the aquatic sectors. Tom gulped. Would he rescue Raphyl too? Or should he allow Raghael and Mirrie to go ahead with the original plan and free him legitimately? He hadn't quite decided yet. He did not want to jeopardise Raphyl's chance of genuine liberty, but equally he did not relish the notion that he was to undertake the mission alone.

Tom studied the intricate diagram and instructions some more, trying to drink in the hard-to-swallow directions. He followed his prospective route with a finger, which eventually arrived at its destination: the final chamber. He gulped again. For in this utmost secret of chambers, was what had been hiding, waiting, for centuries: the spaceship which Tom would have to fly by himself in order to escape.

# CHAPTER 30

There was one more rotation until the next prisoner transporter ship left for Porriduum to arrive in time for the next solar eclipse. The page which had been devoured on a daily basis by the young human was now wrinkled and tear stained. Tom was sure that he knew it now, but he could not help but feel apprehensive. He was eating a bowl of some kind of corn cereal he had been served for breakfast, not really tasting it, when he felt the familiar pull of the pherobot guard's pheromone field. His cell door opened and a morose looking Kayleesh was let in. She had come alone.

Tom put his bowl aside and stood up to greet her. Wordlessly, they embraced. As their tears tumbled down their cheeks they joined in a long kiss, arms pulling each other in close. Eventually, Kayleesh pulled away and the beautiful Augtopian simply looked into Tom's eyes. Through her tears she smiled, and Tom smiled back, his heart soaring.

Silently, they sat next to each other on the bed and Tom rested his arm around her shoulder. His heart was doing an impression of an enthusiastic drummer playing in the venue of his chest and Tom was convinced that she was able to hear it. The reality that he had just kissed an alien both amused and comforted him.

*Mum, Dad, I'd like to introduce you to my new girlfriend – did I mention that she was an alien?*

"What are you laughing at?" Kayleesh asked, wiping away the remainder of her tears.

"Nothing," Tom grinned at her and planted a kiss on her lips. She smiled back.

"I can't believe that you're leaving tomorrow," Kayleesh sighed. "What am I going to do without you? What if you...?"

"...can't make it back?" he was finishing her sentences already. "Don't worry about that. I know the details of the document Raghael produced for me as well as I know the express cuisine menu!" He laughed in an attempt cover his uncertainty.

"But it's a touch more complicated than the express cuisine menu," Kayleesh laughed and shook her head.

"I know," Tom sighed. "But don't worry about me. My brain is fully equipped with the knowledge to escape back to you." He touched her lightly on the nose. He wasn't sure whether he was trying to convince Kayleesh or himself.

"Is there anything I can help you with? Anything at all? I feel so helpless."

"No." Tom shook him head. "Unless, you want to fly a spaceship for me. That's the part I'm most dreading. I've never even driven a car!"

"Isn't it automated?"

"To some extent, but I still have to get it in motion. It's been sitting deep within the crust of the planet for centuries."

"It's evident that Raghael and Mirrie have confidence that you can succeed. Otherwise they wouldn't have told you all of this."

"Maybe."

The pair talked for the rest of the hour until the pherobot guard appeared to escort Tom's visitor away. Tom wished that he was able to walk freely about the station as Nathan had. But Nathan had only been kept in for questioning which had warranted more lenient treatment. Whereas Tom's situation had meant that the cell was acting as a holding cell before his imminent trip.

Kayleesh had assured and reassured Tom that he was capable of carrying out the task set before him. She believed that Tom could easily endure the conditions on Porriduum until it was time to make his move and that he'd succeed in his escape. Her words had comforted him and almost made him believe it himself. But it was another sleepless night for Tom.

Glaring down at his red tag as though it was the beginning of some unwanted disease, Tom Bowler shuffled through the station to the docking bay, escorted by an army of policing Greys. There were half a dozen other convicted civilians bound for the same destination. Head bowed down, heart racing, he made the journey in silence.

"You have five kroms to say your goodbyes," barked one of the police officers on their arrival. "Then we will escort you onto the ship where you will be searched."

Tom looked up for the first time and saw that Kayleesh and Nathan were standing next to the ghastly prisoner transporter ship. Hyganty, Frarkk and Raphyl's parents were behind them and then Tom noticed that Mayty Reeston, his colleague and fellow Spotoon team member, had also come to wave him off on his sorry trip. Mayty wasn't the only team member who had come to support him, for team captain Ghy Hasprin was there too, as well as the rest of Hasprin's Legion. His vision became blurry with tears.

Only his closest friends knew about his plan to escape the prison planet. It was too dangerous for too many people to have knowledge of it. Consequently, Hasprin's Legion looked sorrier than they would have had they lost a match against the Radiakkans; they had in a sense. It wasn't very often that Mayty's broad grin was in the upturned position. Ransel led the team in a salute by cocking their ears at their departing player. Tom returned the gesture. A lump began to cultivate in his throat, making swallowing arduous.

He was pleased that he had such a solid group of friends, but seeing them all together with their pitiful expressions, amplified his shame.

"Make sure you're back before the next season starts," Ghy said, trying to stay cheerful. But his broken voice betrayed him. He gave a false cough; his tough exterior having been shattered. Tom had rather neglected his sport in recent weeks, with his adventures on Radiakka. But he appreciated the fact that his team had made the effort to join together on this occasion. Hyganty and Frarkk both simply nodded at him, allowing him to spend his precious final words on his closest companions.

"Sorry about this, bud," Tom managed.

"I can't believe you're abandoning me again," Nathan teased. "Don't worry about me – Phelmer has arranged an interview for me with Tyrander for a temporary position at the express cuisine while you're er… while you're away."

"That's good," Tom forced a smile.

Kayleesh flew forwards and gave him a hug that neither of them wanted to end. He pulled her close, the aroma of her cinnamon-scented hair pleasantly filling his nasal cavity and promptly finding a place in his memory for the long days ahead without her that would follow. All too soon, she broke away and the prisoners were led onto the ship, fated for Porriduum.

Tom longed for the quarters aboard the Submian ship - spacious, comfortable and, above all, clean. Sitting on the floor in the cramped compartment, on the transporter Tom pulled his knees into his chest. He had been stripped of his timepiece on entry to the ship and had been frisked for any undesirable items he may have on his person.

He felt utterly alone.

The droning and creaking of the craft did little to comfort him. He occupied himself by ruminating over the plan in his head. He knew that first he would need to wait until the next starquake before he could activate stage one of the plan. According to Mirrie, glitches in the stability of the entire Gorgon Ray security system occurred during these starquakes. But they were difficult to predict and even if a prisoner had been fortunate to get through a cell wall during one of these glitches, then they would promptly be caught and re-incarcerated. Unless they knew something more. Unless they knew where the glitches were most apparent – the weakest section of the entire complex, in sector two's dedicated hospital ward. Then he'd wait until the right moment. According to Raghael's calculations, the next glitch would be on the seventh rotation of his term on Porriduum. After that he would have to wait another forty-eight rotations.

Once through the crucial wall, he would then need to progress to the next, and most bizarre, stage of the plan. This stage seemed to Tom like a strange parody of a computer game puzzle, for this part of the plan desired him to prise makeshift tools from the far wall of the staff room; a wall decorated in a lattice of shapes which the Truxxian couple had assured the builders and project managers had been crucial part of the design. It had been imperative that the lattice remained present to ensure the safety and hygiene of the department. However, the wall pattern had served only to be ornamental as an essential part of the jigsaw of their potential escape plan. The quirky shape of the utensils had remained locked in Tom's memory of the drawing; one had borne some resemblance to a starfish; the other a crescent moon. Once he had the correct utensils, the next part of the plan involved using the crescent–shaped implement in a matching slot to enter a concealed exit and then… and then what? Where was he to go next? His mind was suddenly, and terrifyingly, as vacant as a blank parchment.

# CHAPTER 31

Tom was unreservedly panic-stricken. Suddenly, the door to his holding cell thumped open.

"All right, human," grunted an amply proportioned Truxxian. "It is time for you to make your final call before we leave."

"You mean – you mean we haven't left the docking bay yet?"

"We've only just got the last of the prisoners on board and re-fuelled the tank. Why? Are you in some sort of hurry to get to prison?" The Truxxian roared with laughter.

"No, of course not," Tom burst. "But isn't it a bit odd to be offering final calls when I've only just said my goodbyes?"

"Not all prisoners are lucky enough to have had their nearest kin on the station. You had quite a little farewell party back there. If you'd rather forfeit your call, then that can be arranged." The Truxxian made to leave.

"No, of course not!" Tom called out.

"I thought as much," the Truxxian grinned, and licked his lips, as though he was enjoying a rather tasty cream cake. "You may use the general communicator to call your next of kin."

Technically, Tom's next of kin would have been his mother or father. But he knew that contacting them would be a wasteful use of this one chance he had. As much as he longed to speak to them in this moment of lonesomeness, he knew that it wasn't the advice of his own parents which was going to help him. He couldn't ask to speak to Raghael and Mirrie directly, as their identities had not yet been made official on the station and he couldn't remember whether they had been wearing timepieces.

"Please can I speak to Kayleesh, my friend on TSS?"

"The girl you held in your arms mere minutes ago?"

"Yes."

"Very well," the Truxxian sighed. He tapped away at a small grey device before holding it out at arm's length for Tom to pluck from his long, lilac fingers. The device didn't have the same look of a timepiece and was the first communication device of its kind Tom had seen. It was a simple box-type affair, with a basic speaker and microphone. Before Tom could figure out how the Truxxian had managed to patch him through, he heard Kayleesh's voice, clear as diamond.

"Tom!"

The Truxxian shook his head, sighed, and left the chamber.

"Hi, Kayleesh. I need to urgently speak with Raghael or Mirrie. Are they there?" he hissed into the microphone.

"Oh, charming!"

"I'm sorry Kayleesh, it's just I don't have much –"

"I know darling, I understand. I was just having dinner with them while they comforted me. Here." Kayleesh's soft tones faded and the gruff tones of Raphyl's father replaced them.

"Tom, is everything all right? I mean, apart from being destined for Porriduum of course."

"I can't remember a crucial stage of the plan – after I escape through the concealed entrance in the hospital kitchen, where do I go next? I've been racking my brain trying to picture that section of the diagram, but it's just blank!"

"You're panicking, Tom. It's all in there somewhere – stop *trying* to remember and *remember.*"

"That's not helping!" Tom tried not to speak above a whisper. He prayed that there were no cameras in his temporary cell and that the device wasn't bugged. But why should they be suspicious of him? After all, they believed he was merely exchanging sweet sentiments with his loved one. Tom tried to reason with himself.

*It isn't as though I am a class one prisoner. I've been arrested for copying music, not bank notes. It's not as though I've killed anyone.*

"All right Tom, calm down. All you need to do is follow the passage down to the left. Now, it will be dark, unless the builders of that particular section took the initiative to add lights at a later stage. But after all these years I doubt-"

"Please Raghael," he begged, impatiently.

"So sorry. Where was I?"

*You're not a Grandad recounting an old fairy story, this is important! Hurry up!*

"Ah that was it – follow the passageway for several metres. You will then come to a large metal wheel which will need to be turned in order for you to enter the airlock to the water sector from the bottom of the level."

"Oh, so that's the part with the water – I remember now. So how do I go about getting the breathing apparatus, again?"

"You would have come across the equipment in the hospital ward – oxygen masks are abounding in these sectors."

"And you're certain of this?" Tom's head was thumping. He couldn't take all this in, remember it and stay calm. "After all, you're the architect not the-"

"-Of course, I'm certain. It's logical."

"And crucial – if I'm to succeed." He gulped.

"You will – now, do you remember the next bit?"

"Yes, yes I think I do." Tom nodded, as one does when they are talking on the telephone, although the second person is not able to appreciate the gesture.

At that moment, the Truxxian guard clanged back into the cell to reclaim the device.

"Goodbye then Sweetie," Tom cooed into the mouthpiece, swiftly remembering that he was feigning a final conversation with a loved one. He ended his dialogue with the rather startled Truxxian. "I will miss you."

The guard swiped the device from Tom's grasp and snorted.

"You're not seriously expecting her to wait for you are you?"

"Of course," said Tom, crossly. "She'll be there when I return."

"That's what they all say," he snorted again.

*And my return may be sooner than you think.*

Tom wasn't sure how long he had waited in the holding cell of the prison ship, but his stomach was complaining of the sudden change to a pulpy diet and he was sure that his taste buds were considering imminent evacuation if the situation didn't improve. Everything on board was just so basic. And it was noisy. And lonely.

Tom didn't know whether it was morning or evening when his cell door eventually banged open and the Truxxian guard gestured for him to make his leave. Bleary eyed, having been asleep for some hours, the weary human emerged from the compartment. Tom Bowler was led through endless corridor after corridor, his eyes adjusting to the brightness of the complex after the dimly lit interior of the prisoner transporter craft. Just as the Express Cuisine kitchen chef Jephle had described, the infinitely long corridor lined with cells looked wide and open. It appeared as though any of the inmates could saunter out of their cell as they wished, but Tom knew otherwise. He eyed the vents, which he knew were engaged in pouring the neutron star's deadly beams from ceiling to floor. He shuddered at the frightening notion.

Tom wasn't sure whether it was the result of having been penned in solitary confinement for so long, but he was sure that he recognised one of the guards as they passed along the corridor. The guard expelled the unmistakable odour of the meat delivery man who frequented the express cuisine with fresh supplies. It was not the kind of smell that one could forget. The short, scruffy, wiry-haired creature with his cantankerous expression was inimitable. But what was he doing here? He was dressed in the, albeit ill-fitting, garments of a sentry and conversing with one of the prisoners through the invisible wall. Stranger still, a look of recognition flashed across his face. He then scuttled away, as though he had been caught with his hand in the proverbial biscuit tin. What was he up to? Had he even been there at all or had Tom imagined it? Tom felt the weight of tiredness from broken sleep on his eyes.

After a short journey in a tram carriage, and more long, identical corridors, the sentry accompanying Tom eventually stopped at one of the cells and closed the ceiling vent with a click. An already incarcerated prisoner was lying on the top bunk. He opened his eyes momentarily before rolling over and ignoring both newcomer and guard. Tom's feet stayed stubbornly still, delaying the inevitable.

"It's quite safe to enter, now."

Tom fought his desire to run away and made the final few steps of his journey into the compartment. He was barely inside the cell when he heard the click of the ceiling vent open once more. He scowled at the sentry for he had surely been millimetres away from being fried. The sentry merely offered a mocking grin and paced back along the corridor.

"Interesting plan," Hannond said to his brother, grinning.

"Don't go around grinning like that or the sentries will know that you're up to something," scolded his brother.

"I'm just so happy to see you, I can't *help* grinning!"

Schlomm looked as though he was about to bring up his breakfast.

"I think you've spent too long in the company of that Lymouse," he growled.

"A guard – I mean a real guard is coming!" Hannond hissed.

Schlomm turned and jumped, reflexively, at the sight of a sentry and a recognisable human prisoner pacing down the corridor. He composed himself and walked away briskly, in what he hoped appeared to be a professional manner.

# CHAPTER 32

Three legs dangled down over the edge of the top bunk. A long body followed them, and Tom's cellmate dropped to the floor. The rather sleepy-looking yellow-skinned being blinked at him, cricked his neck and sat down beside him on Tom's bunk.

"Welcome to your new, luxury apartment. I'm Tal."

"I'm Tom," Tom said. He looked about the thinly furnished cell with indifference.

"I was joking about it being a luxury apartment."

"I realised that."

"I expect they'll issue you with prison regulation clothes soon enough. No fancy Wardrobian fields in prison. Your Compsuit is wasted here, I'm afraid."

Clothes were not the front issue in the human's mind at that moment. He merely shrugged. All that he could think about was his escape plan. If he had to take in any more information, names or otherwise, he was fearful that the vital information he needed to retain would be pushed out. He had to stay focussed.

"How long are you going to be here for?" Tal said curtly, "I hope it's not too long. I think I might die of mirth in your captivating company!"

"I'm sorry," Tom turned to him. Two blue eyes shone out of a face which had the complexion of a ripe grapefruit. "I should be chirpier today – what with being thrown in a cell on the worst planet in the galaxy!" he spat. Why was he being so rude to this young man? He realised that he should perhaps have been grateful he hadn't been locked in with a creature that made Baff Bulken look like the sugar plum fairy. He said quietly, "No, I really am sorry. But you don't have to worry about me sharing your cell for long. I aim to be out of here soon enough."

"Pah – have an appeal coming up do you?"

"Not exactly."

"Oh, I see. Don't tell me. You're one of these wannabe escapees," Tal chuckled. "Well this is obviously your first time on this planet, or you'd know it was impossible."

"We'll see."

"Well, false hope is better than no hope I suppose," Tal shrugged. He then said, rather oddly, "Hey Tom, do you see this smile?"

"What?" Tom turned again to look at him to discover that the creature was pointing at his own mouth.

"This smile is because I'm going to be out of here in thirty rotations time. I'll be out of here and on my way back home," he said rather smugly and folded his arms.

Tom smiled back, for if his cell mate was soon to be free anyway, he wouldn't feel guilty about not factoring him into his escape plan. Not that he had originally intended to, but it certainly helped to keep things simple.

"Congratulations. And where exactly is home?"

"Before I came here, I was stationed as a contractor on Radiakka," he said rather proudly.

Tom's stomach lurched at the sound of that word.

Tom got very little sleep that night, his eyes half focussed on the cell opposite, where the occupants were slumbering noisily. But it wasn't the sound of snoring which was keeping him from unconsciousness.

The lights had been dimmed across the entire sector to aid sleep, but still Gorgon's deadly rays, focussed through the vents, were invisible to the naked eye. Tom had learned that Gorgon pulsed radiation was caused by particle acceleration near the magnetic poles. He would exploit his knowledge of magnetism to determine the glitch. Just as his eyelids were finally growing heavy, Tom spotted a tuft of cotton, no doubt from one of the bedsheets, drifting casually towards the baleful fourth wall. He almost jumped out of bed when the tuft burst into a nano-second of fizzing light and then was no more.

On the seventh morning of his residence, Tom awoke to find two bowls of porridge being pushed through the serving hatch section of the Gorgon Ray wall as they had every morning prior. Tal dropped to the floor on his three feet and scooped up a bowl, devoured the contents in seconds clambered back onto his bunk, as he had every morning. Routinely, Tom got to his feet, picked up the other bowl and sat back on the bed, spooning the contents into his mouth. But today was different. Today was the day. According to Raghael and Mirrie's calculations, today was the day that he could enter Phase One of his plan. It was the only day he could enter Phase One. Otherwise he would have many more bowls of porridge to get through before the next opportunity window. He wasn't even sure when that would be for it was already getting hard to keep track of the days in here. He wouldn't know who to ask. He had no one he could ask. During the last few days Tom had felt as though he were behaving suspicious whatever he did, although the only suspect activities he had been engaging in were in his mind. He had continued to ruminate over the plan. He was surprised that holocreatures didn't work on Porriduum. Wouldn't it make more sense to have psychic creatures to impede any potential plans of escape? Perhaps they were so sure that escape was impossible that it was not an issue. Doubts flourished in his cogitations. Perhaps reading the minds of prisoners was against criminals' rights.

That would be more like it, if the system was as flawed as that on Earth, Tom thought. Or maybe the psychic creatures didn't work that way. If they did then they would have discovered Raphyl's innocence instantly.

"You're even quieter than usual," Tal piped up, his legs swinging inches from Tom's head.
"I'm er… I'm not feeling too well." He looked down at his bowl. "In fact, I don't even feel like eating. Do you want the rest of my breakfast?"

A yellow hand appeared momentarily, and Tom's bowl disappeared. After a few moments of slurping, Tal spoke again.

"If it's that bad then you should notify the guard. They'll take you to the hospital."

"I think I might," Tom smiled. Phase One had begun.

"You look perfectly healthy to me." Sentry Ninety-Four eyed Tom, holding his chin in a cold hand.

"He didn't finish his breakfast," Tal called down from his bunk.

"That proves nothing. Not everyone is a gannet like you, Tal," he murmured, without taking his eyes off Tom's face.

"Well… not every illness can be seen," Tom uttered. And then he remembered: his ace card. He could kill two Dragonflies with one stone. "I forgot to inform the guards on entry that I have radiation poisoning. I need to be cleansed of radiation."

"Really?" Sentry Ninety-Four did not sound convinced.

"Yes, it happened while I was on Radiakka. I was exposed to the feet of a swarm of Dragonflies."

"I see. Well it can't do any harm admitting you to the hospital sector as a precautionary measure. But if you're lying, it won't be dragonfly feet you'll be exposed to. It'll be Gorgon's Rays!"

# CHAPTER 33

Tom Bowler climbed out of the glass chamber in which he had been standing for several minutes. He had been found to have been telling the truth about his condition. To Tom's relief, the procedure had been simple and painless. A nurse duly informed him that he had been successfully cleansed from radiation poisoning and led him to a hospital bed where he told him to rest for the remainder of the day.

But Tom was going to be anything *but* resting that afternoon. He lay down and allowed his body to be still, but his mind was racing, and his adrenal glands were working double shifts. Mercifully, the nurse left the room to attend to other patients and Tom was soon alone. Even the other beds in the ward were vacant. He was pleased with the way in which things had panned out thus far. He heard the certainty of Raghael's voice in his mind.

"It's logical."

*It's logical? What had he said before that when we spoke all those days ago? Of course!*

Tom leapt up and reached for the most likely-looking oxygen mask from a rack at the far end of the room. He kept glancing back at the door, paranoia setting in and taking residence in his brain. He crept back to the bed and lay back down. He examined the mask which sat like a dead rubber squid in his hands.

*If I had forgotten to pick up one of these, it would be game over.*

Tom realised that he had to get every stage of the plan exactly right. There was no second life. No cheat codes. And no reset button. This was no game.

Tom could see the kitchen area he needed access to for the next part of the plan. He knew that it was currently unreachable due to the Gorgon Ray wall, while staff were not present. He waited for the inevitable glitch in the weak partition.

And he waited.

As Raghael had predicted, the various metallic medical instruments adorning every wall ever so slightly twitched in unison. It was barely noticeable; Tom would not have detected the disturbance had he not been expecting it. Then, slowly, soundlessly, still on their hooks, the many instruments leaned further and further in the direction of the unstable door. It was only a centimetre or two, but the evidence of the glitch was there. Seconds later, they returned slowly to their original positions. Being alone in the eerie ward with dozens of seemingly possessed implements made Tom feel uneasy.

The activity of the moving instruments reminded Tom of the way in which iron filings behaved when exposed to a powerful magnet. This was the same principle. He dropped to the floor, crawled across the deserted room and over to the doorway to wait for the next glitch. He kept his eyes on a row of stethoscopes, their bells hanging like clock pendulums. The bells twitched and swung maybe a centimetre, and then reset once more. It was almost time.

Just as every hanging, metallic device in the room swung and bowed for a third time, Tom threw the oxygen mask through the gap. To his relief, it survived, unscathed. He smiled at his little victory.

This was it. It was time. He had to go through at the next fissure, or he would be caught, and he'd be stuck here forever. Or fried. And Tom wasn't sure which was worse.

He waited again for the glitch and then… *Now!*

From his crouched position, Tom tumbled through the gap.

He had made it – he was alive!

Before his smug-o-meter overloaded, Tom reminded himself that he had only completed Phase One of the plan. He got up off the cold floor and looked around for the lattice of shapes. Where was it? Then Tom spotted it. It did indeed look like a patterned wall. Now that he saw it for real, up close, he was wholly impressed.

What a clever idea – no one would ever suspect its intended use.

Tom hunted around for the tools he needed - the crescent moon and starfish. He frowned. The oddment of shapes bore very little resemblance to anything familiar. They looked like forms which had been created by a five-year-old let loose with a pastry cutter who had then attached the shapes to a huge cobweb. Eventually, he ran his hands over a form which could pass for a crescent moon and the one bearing the most resemblance to a starfish was a foot or so out of his reach. Jumping up, he managed to snap off the shape in question and pocketed his bounty.

Hannond lay waiting as Jenrothrah Kale the Lymouse slumbered after a particularly heavy Lacbeetle milk binge. He had managed to procure a holdall from one of the guards. It seemed that the guard felt sorry for someone who had the misfortune to be incarcerated with a Lymouse and a tatty canvas bag was small recompense. In the holdall, Hannond planned to store as many gas bubbles as he could from the flatulent Lymouse. He knew that the bubbles were delicate enough to burst when prodded or jabbed, but if he was careful enough, their viscous skin should allow them to rest comfortably together in the bag until needed.

Soon enough, a soundless bubble wobbled up from the sleeping Lymouses's behind and into Hannond's waiting hands.

He imagined what he must look like as he performed this action and hoped that a passing sentry did not spot him. Not because it might scupper his plans, but because of the utter embarrassment it would induce; nobody wished to be renowned for being a fart collector.

The oxygen mask was serving its purpose as Tom swam up through the water level. He only wished it had come equipped with a pair of goggles, for all he could see was a blur of light and dark. He followed the directions from his memory of Raghael's drawing and swam up as far as he could and then ahead towards three apertures in the wall. He took the central tunnel then turned right, then left and was finally faced with two circular heavy-duty doors. One of the doors, he knew, led to the long water corridor which housed the cells on that level. The other led to the next phase of his plan. Tom wasn't used to swimming underwater for prolonged periods. He hadn't engaged in any energetic pursuits since he had left Earth and playing Spotoon hardly counted.

Heaving at the metal ring in the centre of the door on the left, his strength having been sapped from swimming, Tom struggled to budge it even an inch. His strength was suddenly revitalised, however, when he heard the four terrifying words which emanated from his mask.

"Oxygen at ten percent."

Gathering all his drive, Tom Bowler pulled and pulled. Eventually, his hard work was finally rewarded and the door to the airlock gushed open. Once the water had drained away, he reached out and opened the next door which led onto another corridor. Once on the other side of the airlock Tom could finally breathe and see with ease. Exhausted, Tom wished that none of this was real. He wished that it was a just computer game. That way he could save his position, make himself a cup of tea and come back later when he felt refreshed. But, unlike a game avatar, he was drenched through, cold and hungry having given away half of his breakfast to Tal.

The sound of nearing footsteps prompted him to dive into a nearby storage room. He closed the door behind him, dropped the spent oxygen mask to the floor and brushed wet locks out of his eyes. This was where the second tool would need to be implemented. He retrieved the starfish-shaped tool from his sodden pocket and searched the floor for a starfish-shaped recess in the dim light.

It has to be here somewhere!

Tom froze. He wasn't looking for a recess shape in the floor. That had been the purpose of the crescent shape. This one had a different purpose. *What was he supposed to do with it?* Once again, panic was eating away at his memory like Pacman on a white dot munching binge. Soon there would be no white dots.

*Aagh, this isn't a computer game, Tom. This is real. You're inside a real prison planet in soaking wet clothes and in real trouble. Think!*

He turned the shape around in his hand. It glinted, jewel-like. Then he remembered. He wasn't supposed to be standing in the storage room – it didn't lead anywhere. He was supposed to be standing where the guards could see him, out in the corridor. This insane part of the plan required guile, self-belief, and a rather large chunk of bravery.

Tom gulped.

Schlomm Putt was grinning to himself, confident in his brother's success for his portion of the plan. He couldn't fail. Hannond wanted nothing more than to escape, so he *had* to succeed. After all, how difficult could it be, collecting a bag of wind? Even a human could achieve such a task!

He was wandering the corridors, still endeavouring to remain inconspicuous. His mind reverted to his being conned at the games on Sector Thirteen. He scowled at the memory. How could he have been so foolish to have lost such a huge sum of money in such a fashion? He scowled at the thought of the face of the Strellion who had gained from his loss – the creature who had tricked him. Schlomm's pockets were as barren as his heart.

The Glorbian was startled when a door to his immediate left opened and out emerged a human prisoner. The prisoner was dripping wet and he looked just as startled to see him. What should he do? Report him? He didn't have time for this, his priority was Hannond. But if he was seen to be ignoring this would-be escapee then his position as sentry would surely be questioned. Another thought occurred to him - perhaps if he informed on the prisoner there would even be a reward of some kind.

Schlomm looked about him. There were no other guards around. They were alone in the corridor; he was all his.

The human spoke.

"I wonder whether you can help me." He was obviously a very polite human; not your typical convict at all. The boy held out a hand and in its damp palm glistened a single Star Coin.

Or at least it looked like a Star Coin. Schlomm's eyes widened. He had only ever seen three of its kind in his life. If rubber bungs were celebrated on Porriduum then one of these coins could *buy* Porriduum.

"Where did you get that from, prisoner?" he reached up to grab the beguiling artefact, but the boy snatched his hand away before he could touch it. "That is no small change that you have in your possession. Is that a genuine Star Coin?"

"I understand that these coins are worth more than a Porriduum sentry could make in a lifetime. That is how I know that you will not betray my confidence and notify anyone that I am out of my cell. But most importantly I need you to grant me safe passage to Sector Seventeen." *Had this human been rehearsing this line or is it how they spoke on his world?* Schlomm wondered.

The Star Coin would undoubtedly be worth many times more than any reward he would receive for turning the wretched mite in.

"Sector Seventeen? What is on Sector Seventeen that is worth more than that coin?"

"My freedom," he said confidently. He brushed stray, wet hair across his face and out of his eyes and Schlomm could see clearly who the boy was. He gulped.

# CHAPTER 34

Tom Bowler was shaking with both cold and nerves as he approached the guard. He detected the unmistakable odour. He was stunned into silence, for again he was confronted with the gnarled features of the stumpy meat delivery man he had passed in the corridor on his arrival. He was certain of it this time.

The short creature and he seemed to share synchronised realisation as Tom noticed his jaw slacken and his eyes bulge in apprehension. This was no sentry. And if this creature knew that Tom recognised him as the delivery man, then Tom had another bargaining tool.

The "sentry" was visibly quaking, his mouth silently uttering nonsensical words. Gone was the pompous guard; he had been replaced by a gibbering jellyfish. Tom prayed that this creature would be fooled into believing that the shape was in fact a real Star Coin. For Raghael had assured him that few could resist such precious treasure.

The unlikely duo journeyed through the complex; their jaunt having already taken three times as long as it should on account of Schlomm's lack of local knowledge. Tom noticed that One Four One was frowning.

"If you don't mind me saying, you don't look like a man who's about to become the wealthiest person on the planet," Tom whispered.

"If you must know, I was concentrating – I am trying to figure out the most direct route."

"You don't seem to know your way around the prison too well," Tom stifled a laugh. "We've passed this door three times now; I recognise the scuff marks on the wall."

One Four One gave an audible sigh. He was definitely no sentry. "Look, I might not be able to find sector seventeen straight away, you bothersome human, but once we do find it then you will need me in order to access it. So, unless you're going to be of any help, then keep quiet."

"Don't you have a map?"

"If I had a map we would be there by now, wouldn't we?" Schlomm said through gritted teeth.

"Couldn't you try and get one?" Tom knew that he was teasing the poor creature, but he was enjoying himself. It was such a luxury to be free from the cell.

"It's not that easy. Believe me I've tried!"

Before they lapped the sector again, Schlomm tried a different turning and at the end of another long passageway the two stumbled across a tram station. The sign on the wall read: To restricted zones. Sentries 1 – 150 only. Tom noticed Schlomm look proudly at the number on his uniform and he smiled at Tom, triumph dancing in his eyes.

The sentry imposter approached the door which opened onto an empty tram. This was all going so well. Too well, perhaps?

"Sector Seventeen," Schlomm requested. The tram began its smooth journey, gathering speed. Within minutes, they had arrived at their destination.

Tom Bowler's suspicions were confirmed; things had been going too well. For he and the Glorbian crook were greeted at sector seventeen by a high-ranking sentry.

Sentry Eleven, a bulky creature with tiny eyes which would be better suited on an ageing potato, glared at Tom.

"Halt! You are not permitted to be in this sector, prisoner."

"He's with me, it's OK," Schlomm padded around from behind the human and matched Sentry Eleven's glare.

"I don't care if he's here with a Wheylandian politician, he is not allowed to be in this area."

"Believe me, I'd rather not be here," lied Tom. "I was quite happy, enjoying my morning in my cell when I was whisked away and told I was being introduced to a new punishment regime in this region of the..."

"Silence, prisoner! I have no idea what you're talking about! And what was the first portion of this new punishment regime? Being dunked in the tub in the sanitation room?" Sentry Eleven sniffed his wet shoulder.

Tom looked down at his dripping clothes. He couldn't see a way out of the situation. Sentry Eleven was obviously too clever to be fooled so easily.

"What is going on here?" A pale-faced humanoid hollered from the far end of the passageway. The humanoid, apparently Sentry Nine, quickly joined the small gathering. "What is all this about, Eleven, and why did you allow this prisoner off the tram?"

"I am currently resolving the issue," Sentry Eleven assured him. "This incompetent guard and his prisoner were about to get back on the tram."

"You can join us on our tram ride if you wish, Sentry Nine." Schlomm said.

*What is he doing?* thought Tom.

"Where is it you're off to? Sector *Thirteen?*" Schlomm remarked.

"What?" puffed Sentry Nine. And then a look of realisation. "Oh!"

What was going on? Did the Glorbian know something about this guard? Whatever it was, Sentry Nine's already pallid face grew

even paler.

"I'm sure a high-ranking guard such as yourself would not need to frequent the laundry in person, or at least the room that..."

"I'm sure I can handle this situation, Eleven," Sentry Nine interrupted. "If you'd like to go on your lunch break I can take this from here."

"But..."

"Just *go,* Eleven."

The guard with the tiny eyes shrugged and stepped into the tram which immediately left.

"I do not appreciate being blackmailed!"

"And I do not appreciate being robbed by a crooked Strellion!" Schlomm barked.

"Fiddle you, did he? I'm sorry about that. You can never be too careful with Strellions, can you?"

"Yes well, you can make it up to me by granting us passage into this sector."

"Fine. You have a deal. But can I ask the purpose of your little visit? This is merely the staff quarters for high-ranking staff."

"You can ask me, yes. But I am not going to give you the satisfaction of an answer. And Nine - you haven't seen this prisoner in this sector, all right? Just as I haven't seen *you* in Sector Thirteen gambling like the convicts you are supposed to be punishing!"

"That was lucky," Tom said.

"Luck had nothing to do with it. And luck certainly has nothing to do with gambling. Not in this stinking..." One Four One growled, bitterly. "Anyway, where next, human?"

"Er, you can leave me here. I only needed to get through the other side of that door."

"Oh no you don't," One Four One warned. "If I've helped you get this far and you are making a bid for freedom, I want in. Or, er... out."

*What should I do?* Tom didn't particularly want the company of a grumpy Glorbian on his journey home. It would be like being stuck in a lift with a flatulent Rottweiler.

"Erm... well I need to get underground."

"We're already underground. We're deep underneath the molten surface of this rotten planet!" Schlomm scoffed.

"I know, I'd er... I'd rather not think about that," Tom shuddered. "But I need to get to the bowels of Sector Seventeen. That's where the, er... that's where I need to get to."

Tom did not want to give too much away. He didn't know how far he could trust this imposter. He didn't even know what One Four One was doing here, although he was pleased that their encounter had got him this far.

Schlomm growled.

"Hmm, well let's get going then. Do you actually know where you're going, you strange boy?"

"I think so." Tom scanned through the plans in his mind's eye. "Why are you here anyway? Who would want to disguise themselves as a sentry?"

"I'm here for my brother," Schlomm huffed.

"Your *brother?* Does he play Spotoon by any chance?"

"Yes, how did you know that?"

Hannon Putt had befriended a Blandart beast. It hadn't been easy. Prisoners on Porriduum weren't granted time for exercise or recreation. They were only permitted half an hour a day in the sanitation block and the rest of the time was spent in the cell. With only the company of a depressed Lymouse by day and a moment of a guard's time at mealtimes, Hannond was pretty restricted, socially.

Placid Hannond was not a violent creature by nature, but he could see no other way of being moved out of the cell. And Jenrothrah Kale had been particularly irritating that day. His whining and fretting had driven Hannond to the very edge of sanity and pushed him right off into the ocean of spontaneous aggression.

The Lymouse had been slumped in the corner of the cell, still nursing his head when the guard had come to escort the Glorbian to another cell.

"I'm so sorry," the ever-whimpering creature had sobbed. "I'm sorry I drove you to this. I never meant to."

"You really are pathetic, aren't you, Kale?" The burly Sentry One Seven Three had shook his head. "Are you sure you don't wish to visit the hospital ward to be checked over, Kale?"

"I don't deserve to crumple the bedsheets of the hospital ward. I'm only a poor Lymouse. I..."

"Very well. You can't say I didn't offer," the guard had snorted before marching Hannond off down the passageway.

The nature of Hannond's crime had resulted in his transfer to another sector. He was now a Class Three prisoner. The chance of being incarcerated with a Blandart Beast was much higher amongst this class of prisoners. And he had been in luck. A vacant bed in the company of a *particularly* beastly looking Blandart Beast was awaiting his arrival.

He wasn't a very pleasant person to be around. Hannond had to make a special effort to appeal to his benevolent side. And the benevolent side of a Blandart Beast was hard to find. He thought that perhaps offering him his supper would be a good start. And he was right.

Following the map in Tom Bowler's memory, he weaved through the corridors of sector seventeen. Notably easier to navigate around than the rest of the complex, he soon found the room above where he needed to be. The undercover sentry, whose name he had now learnt to be Schlomm Putt, was still in his company.

The room in which they had found themselves was a sanitation unit.

*What is it with me and toilets? At least it's not occupied.*

Tom reached in his pocket for the crescent-shaped tool. He felt around the dusty floor for the slot, which was less obvious than the first one had been. His fingers eventually met with a recess and Tom slotted in the crescent-shaped key. A mechanism clicked compliantly, and a section of the floor slid across. Unfortunately, it was the section of floor on which Schlomm had been standing and he dropped like a stone through the opening.

"You stupid human!" Tom heard him call through the darkness.

"Sorry!" Tom called down after him. "And I didn't ask you to come with me!"

"Well I'm here now. Come on. I'll see if I can find a light source. And I still haven't had that coin star!"

Tom lowered himself through the opening and landed safely. It was then that he noticed the ladder. Tom shrugged.

Schlomm had not managed to locate a light switch, but as the trap door slid closed above them, they were confronted with the glorious sight of a gleaming, twinkling spaceship.

Tom stood, gaping at the craft before him. He had seen a huge variety of spaceships since he had left Earth, but he was still filled with awe whenever he was confronted with a new one. This ship was different because it was *his* ship; or at least, he would be at the helm for one journey.

It amazed Tom that the ship - this glimmering, spherical craft - had been hidden away underground for the entire lifetime of the complex. Mirrie had explained to him that only craft produced using a rare metallic element found only on planet Porriduum could survive the journey through the molten layers. This ship was made from the same substance as the prisoner transporter ships. He considered this as he circled the small ship, tracing the hull with his fingers. The exterior was smooth, cool, enticing.

"Stop fondling the thing and climb aboard!" Schlomm barked. "And you can hand me over my payment while you're at it."

Tom pretended that he had not heard this last remark and continued to occupy himself with the business of examining the ship. He was attempting to locate the door. He finally located the entrance and the keypad, which could only be activated using the combination code with which Tom had been entrusted.

A, Z, 1, 5, B. Tom's heart was thumping as he punched the corresponding keys. *Please work. Pleas work!* After a tantalising moment, the door slid open and a short ramp descended. Tom smiled to himself.

"I think that that was pretty impressive, considering the thing's been sitting here dormant for hundreds of years."

"You are too easily impressed," Schlomm spat.

Tom climbed aboard, his stumpy follower clambering after him. Tom whistled, marvelling at the sleek interior. He was almost spellbound by the new-car fragrance of the interior, drinking in the vision of blinking lights and monitors. This was his *idea* of a spaceship.

Tom eagerly took to the helm, an intellibelt sliding across his lap as he tried to make himself comfortable in the seat which had been designed for a long-limbed Truxxian. *He had reached the final phase of the plan.*

In all his wonderment, Tom had almost forgotten that the Glorbian was still present, but the growing stench in the enclosed space soon reminded him.

"Is that coin star still burning a hole in your pocket?"

Tom pulled the star coin shaped ornament from his pocket and placed it in Schlomm's sweaty palm. He waited for him to leave, but it didn't happen.

"I am now without a spaceship. And you are without someone who knows how to fly a spaceship."

"It's automated," Tom told him. "I don't need to know how to fly it. And don't be so presumptuous – I may be a very good helmsman for all you know."

"Either way, I'm coming with you!"

"You are, are you?" Tom was getting rather irritated by the creature now.

"And so is my brother."

"OK, you have helped me out today. And Hannond does seem like gentle sort." Tom gave in. "But you'll have to be quick in fetching him. Timing is critical as the window of opportunity isn't very big." Tom decided that he didn't have the heart not to allow the brothers on board. Schlomm was cantankerous, self-serving and irritating but Tom was considerate, thoughtful and charitable. Plus, he was feeling less confident about a solo journey back to Truxxe. Even the company of Glorbians was better than no company at all. Especially when faced with the vastness of space. And the idea of being utterly alone out there was a terrifying notion indeed.

"Fire her up then and I'll go and 'escort' the prisoner to this escape pod of yours," grinned Schlomm.

Tom leaned forward and pulled the single lever marked Start.

But to his utter horror, the ship did the exact opposite. The interior lights blinked out one by one and he was left sitting in darkness.

# CHAPTER 35

Nathan Reed had completed his second week at the Express Cuisine at TSS. He had taken to the job easily and busied himself in his work and in the company of his colleagues. But whether he was at work, at Bar Six Seven or playing a game of Spotoon, he was unable to stop thinking about Tom. This was partly because he was doing all the things that Tom usually did on Truxxe, so it was his own fault, but he couldn't help but worry. Nathan's old school mate had never used to be particularly adventurous. He hadn't even walked to school by himself until he was thirteen. And now he was light years away, stranded on a planet dedicated to holding the criminal population of two galaxies. Tom had come a long way in the last few months; literally. And not all of it was for the better.

Nathan and Kayleesh, pay packets in hand, had joined Raghael and Mirrie in Bar Six Seven that evening. The older Truxxians didn't seem particularly comfortable in a venue predominately occupied by younger people who weren't bothered by loud music, but they were too polite to complain.

"I've worked it out," Raghael hollered over the lively music. "By my calculations, if Tom has been following the plan correctly, then he should be on his way home by now."

"Really? You mean, *right now?*" Kayleesh gushed. Nathan could almost see the excitement bursting out of her. He hadn't seen that smile for a while.

"How long will his journey back take him?" asked Nathan.

"From our perspective, he should be due to arrive here in two rotations."

"He is so brave," Kayleesh squealed.

"I don't envy his situation," said Nathan. "But it is all pretty exciting. I wish I was in that spaceship with him."

"So do I," sighed Kayleesh.

"I bet you do!"

If Kayleesh could blush, Nathan thought that she would be doing so at that moment. The two of them laughed.

"Maal, I need your assistance," Schlomm Putt said, adjusting his breathing apparatus. He looked through the thick atmosphere of sector four at the prisoner. "For some reason I've got myself involved in the escapades of a dumb Earthling. An Earthling who was my ticket out of here - almost. But now seems that his intricate little escape plan has failed."

"Escape plans always fail. No one has ever escaped." Maal bared his three sets of teeth, non-threateningly. It was difficult for him not to bare his teeth. They were positively overflowing out of his mouth.

"But this human insisted that his plan was fool proof. Well, more fool him," he growled.

"Sentry, your words mean nothing. You will have to explain these supposed means of escape, or I can't help you. And if I *can* help you, my consultancy fee will increase to ten crates of Glorbian whiskey," he added, slyly.

"Ten crates? Very well." Schlomm sighed. He explained to Maal about the secret spaceship which had been hidden beneath the prison, how he had learned of its special properties, how it was able to survive a journey through the molten crust of a hostile planet. He explained that when Tom had pulled the start lever that the power to the entire ship had been extinguished. "We deduced that due to the centuries of dormancy, the detonator had expired, meaning that there's not enough power to keep the cockpit illuminated, let alone achieve escape velocity."

"So your little ship needs a boost eh?"

"Exactly."

"Sentry One Four One – or whoever you are – how is the original plan coming along?"

"The original plan?"

"Kaboom!"

"Ka – oh! Of course!" Schlomm slapped a palm to his goldfish bowl helmet. "Kaboom! Of course!"

"I thought you were never coming back," Tom called out as he spotted Schlomm descending into the secret chamber.

"You have less patience than a Glorbian!" a gruff voice shouted back.

Through the dimly lit chamber, Tom was startled to see that the kindred Glorbians were accompanied by a huge, hulking creature with all the grace and poise of a disorientated elephant. Unable to manage the ladder it had simply taken the route that Schlomm had taken on his first drop sown. As he stood up, Tom saw that its face had pug-like qualities, as though he had had met with a spade wielding battalion. At first, Tom thought he was wearing an over-sized suit of armour but then he saw that the newcomer was actually harbouring an immense shell on its back. Rough and rock-like, quite unlike the relative smoothness of a tortoise shell, the thing looked as though it was weighing the creature down. His expression of discomfort suggested this too.

"Don't look so startled," Schlomm snapped. "He's not joining us. He's merely going to solve our little problem."

"Is this going to take long?" The beast growled. "And when do I get my star coin?"

"It won't take long," Schlomm said through gritted teeth.

"What's going on?" Tom asked. "I thought you were going to find a way of starting the detonator. Or is this... gentleman... going to fix it for us?" he asked, carefully.

"Oh the detonator isn't usable. It's old. Dead. I told you that. No, no, no I have brought us a new detonator."

"Oh. Well, where is it?"

"Here," Schlomm grinned. He gestured towards the beast.

"What do you mean?" Tom stood up. What was happening? He knew he shouldn't have trusted the undercover sentry. Schlomm ignored him, however.

"Come on Hannond, bring your rucksack with you." He led the prisoners around to the back of the ship. Tom followed. "What are you doing, human? You need to be at the helm. You need to be ready!"

"I want to know what you're doing, though," Tom protested.

"In that case you'd better be ready to run when I say."

Tom nodded.

"Hannond, start loading the shell."

"What's going on here?" The Blandart beast bellowed.

"Did I really need to collect so many of these?" Hannond queried. Tom watched in awe as Hannond proceeded to reach into a bag and pull out what looked like a glutinous bubble.

"Of course. The extra bubbles were good cushioning for the one that we will end up using. Besides, you never know, you might end up bursting one or-" And right on cue, Hannond's hoary skin was too much for the bubble which he had in his hand and suddenly the thing was no more. All that remained was a sticky residue and a ghastly smell.

"Argh, what is that?" Tom covered him mouth, afraid that he was about to be sick. He stepped back inside the ship to escape the stench. He began coughing and retching, as did the rest of them.

As the odour dissipated, the four gathered together again.

"Sorry about that," Hannond said, reaching for another bubble. "These orbs contain the expelled gasses of a Lymouse."

"They what?" Tom gasped. He eyed the second bubble and took a few steps back, hand to his nose in preparation. "Expelled gases? They're bottled farts? Why are you carrying around a bag of…"

"They're to fuel the detonator," Hannond explained, quite seriously.

"I see..." Tom said, not quite seeing.

Tom gaped as he watched the strange Hannond coolly climb onto his brother's round shoulders. Was he about to perform some kind of trick? The beast evidently couldn't feel the weight of the Glorbian's hand through his thick shell as the bubble was slotted into what Tom saw was a recess in the creature's back.

"I suggest you hold on to the ship," Schlomm told the beast. "And that star coin will soon be yours." The beast obeyed. Tom wasn't sure that he would have taken such a risk, even with the promise of a real star coin. Still perched on his brother's shoulders, Hannond reached in his pocket and a look of disappointment swept over him as he pulled out an empty hand.

"Erm... you don't happen to have a light do you, Pebbles?"

*Pebbles?* Tom sniggered to himself. Is that some kind of pet name Hannond has for the beast? Or even worse, was it his real name?

"Um... yes," Pebbles fumbled in his prisoner uniform trousers and handed him a long match. "But what do you want it for?"

"I think now is the time for you to get inside the ship, human."

Tom didn't need to be asked twice.

The explosion was even more horrific than Tom had imagined. He could feel the vibration of the escape pod as it burrowed out, cracking through the thick mantle of the planet and burst out into the shadow of the eclipsing moon. Tom was aware that the automated path of the ship was moving them along an arc of safety as they travelled in parallel with the moon, their shield. His teeth rattled in his skull as they juddered out of orbit, debris clanking around the hull of the ship as they made their escape. The timing for this final stage of the plan had been critical. They hadn't yet been atomised, which was always a good sign.

Eventually, the din quietened down, and Tom opened his eyes again. He saw that the two brothers were locked in a terrified embrace. They too opened their eyes and quickly parted.

Hannond seemed to be singing, although Tom could no longer understand his words, due to the absence of an ALSID unit.

Schlomm appeared to be actually dancing about the ship.

Tom began to laugh. For he was now free.

# CHAPTER 36

"I wonder how soft a landing this is going to be," Schlomm mused.

"As soft as Pebbles," Hannond mumbled.

"What? Do you think he's still out there?"

"If he held on tight enough there is a possibility, yes," Hannond said casually. "If Blandart Beasts can hold their breath anyway!"

The escape pod neared Truxxe, its hull rising in temperature as it passed through the atmosphere of the planetoid. It soon cooled down, however, as it skimmed the surface of one of Truxxe's few oceans. Pebbles skimmed across the water as he clung onto the hull. By this point however, he was not as much clinging on to the ship, as embedded into the hull itself.

The craft eventually came to a stop on the sandy shore, the waves lapping at both ship and beast.

Tom and the Glorbians disembarked, wobbly-legged, onto the surface of the eternally dark planet. Unable to communicate with the others, Tom simply watched the brothers as they babbled to each other in their own language. He was soon distracted by the grunting of the giant beast who was proceeding to extract himself from a rather large dent in the side of the escape pod.

Feeling guilty, Tom attempted to help him, but his efforts were not enough to prise off the creature which had barnacled himself to the ship. He eventually managed to free himself, however, and Tom saw that his face was flatter as ever. His entire shell was scorched, and his prisoner uniform had been burnt off completely.

Tom was filled with both pity and mirth as the strangely robust and naked being lumbered away. He was free. And for the most part, safe. Tom didn't call after him, as he assumed Pebbles wouldn't be fluent in English.

Tom noticed a cluster of glow rocks. He looked up and realised that he knew where he was. As the brothers danced and made ominous noises at each other, Tom made his way to Crossvein Tourist Centre, which Tom knew was barely a few miles from TSS.

Exhausted, but elated, Tom finally stumbled into the brightly lit interior of TSS. Judging by the artificial lighting, Tom estimated that it was post mid sun. His friends would still be in the Express Cuisine.

With a sheepish grin on his face, Tom Bowler made his way to his workplace. He ducked past Mayty Reeston, who was cleaning a particularly messy table, and sidled up to the counter.

"I really fancy a nice, big, juicy burger!" he grinned.

"Tom!" Kayleesh squealed. She ran round the counter, threw her arms around him in delight and pulled him in for a long hug. He wrapped his arms around her and enjoyed the moment he had waited so long for.

"Hey, bud!" Nathan cried out as he leapt over the counter, almost knocking a disgruntled looking customer over in the process. He joined his friends in their embrace, squeezing them both tightly.

"Hey!" Tom laughed and broke away.

"Bud, you look awful!" Nathan made a face. "I think you need more than one burger to fatten you up a bit." He grinned.

"Hey Tom!" Mayty Reeston realised that his friend had sneaked past him and ran to join them. He made Hasprin's Legion's team gesture with one waggling ear and a broad grin spread across his round, orange face. His team-mate was back. "I propose a company outing to bar Six Seven."

"I can't thank you enough," Tom gushed, giving both Raghael and Mirrie a hug, in turn. "Your plan actually worked!"

"Don't sound so surprised," Raghael said, a little offended.

"Oh, sorry, I didn't doubt for a krom that it wouldn't but-"

"Oh, come on Raghael," Mirrie said softly. "The boy has been through a lot. He should be congratulated. Well done Tom!" She turned to Tom. "I assume that you landed safely in the waters of the northern continent? Did everything go according to plan? Was the take off a smooth one? Was the underwater deck-"

"Mirrie!" Raghael interjected. "Cease with the questioning. The boy has been through enough.!" The couple laughed. "Anyway, I'm sure Tom would be more interested in speaking to our son than us."

Moments later, Raphyl appeared, struggling with arms full of beverages as he reached their usual table.

"Tombo!" Raphyl almost dropped his bounty in surprise. He set the drinks down carefully and said, "I'll go and get you one of those strange-tasting drinks that you and Nathan like."

Tom grinned. In fact, he couldn't stop grinning. He invited Kayleesh to sit on his knee and he held her close. He kissed her on the forehead, fondly. She smiled at him.

Tom Bowler finally had all of his friends around him once more. Well, most of them.

"Tom," a voice called out, as though far away but strangely close. He sat bolt upright.

"What is it?" Kayleesh asked, clutching her boyfriend tightly to stop herself from tumbling onto the floor.

"Did you hear it? Someone called my name." He stood up. He was certain he had recognised the voice. But who was it? And then he remembered. It was the voice of Gracer Menille. Tom turned round and was confronted with the stocky form of the flame-haired, gilled alien.

"Tom," her voice was clearer now. More solid. Although there was something about her presence which suggested that she wasn't.

"Gracer!" Tom reached out to hug her. He was being very generous with his hugs today. He had even given the strange Submian creatures a quick squeeze, such was his jubilant mood. But his arms passed straight through Gracer. Of course, she was using a holoceiver. "Gracer, how nice of you to come and see us." He grinned. A glimmer of uncertainty danced about her face. "Don't worry, I'm fine. I'm back on Truxxe – look!" he laughed and took a swig of his lager.

"I know you're on Truxxe. I *dialled* Truxxe," she said. Yet a smile still refused to appear on her lips.

"Are you worried that I'm an escapee – that I haven't done the time for my punishment and that I might be thrown back on that planet again?" Tom asked. He was worried about the inevitability of this happening. He had no idea what the next stage of his plan would be. He was just enjoying the moment while he could; in the company of his friends with real food and real drinks. Even if it was just for a short time.

"I don't think that will still be an issue." Gracer bit her lip.

"What do you mean? Oh, you work in the Parliamentary Building don't you? Have the Radiakkan government changed their laws again? Is illegal data copying now... legal?" he chuckled, still riding his high like a surfer of the crest of a ten-feet-high wave.

There was a moment of ominous silence. No one spoke.

"There's something that you need to know," Gracer's hologram looked at each of them. "Tom, listen to me."

"I'm listening," he said.

"Do you remember when I told you about Radiakka II? That the Radiakkans are planning to invade another planet?"

"Yes."

And then the ten-foot wave came crashing down over him.

"They've announced which planet they're going to invade." She paused before saying solemnly, "Tom, they're planning on invading Earth."

# ALSO BY RUTH MASTERS

## THE TRUXXE TRILOGY

Three novels following the adventures of Tom Bowler, a human who finds himself working in an intergalactic service station during his gap year. He discovers the secrets of the planetoid Truxxe, traverses the galaxy to rescue his alien friend from the prison planet Porriduum and ultimately defends the earth against an alien invasion.

A cast of colourful aliens good and bad, fantastic alien worlds and witty dialogue make this trilogy a great read for any sci-fi fan!

Vol 1: All Aliens Like Burgers
Vol 2: Do Aliens Read Sci-Fi?
Vol 3. When Aliens Play Trumps

## AUTOGRAPH HUNTER SERIES

A pair of "paraquels", each covering similar events, from the perspective of different characters. In both books, attendees at the same sci-fi convention happen across a real working time machine, and set off on autograph-hunting missions through time.

The two pairs of friends cross paths occasionally, with Rosemary and Joanne intriguingly being one step ahead of Alistair and Jeremy. Along the way they meet the great and the good of history, from Shakespeare to the inventor of the modern toilet. Friendships are tested and life will never be the same again…

Vol 1: Extreme Autograph Hunters
Vol 2: Ultimate Autograph Hunters

## BELISHA BEACON & TABITHA TURNER

Tabitha Turner is a complaints executive from contemporary Birmingham. Belisha Beacon is a celebrity DJ working on the illustrious Möbius Strip, orbiting the planet Hayfen IV, 400 years in the future.

Inexplicably finding themselves inhabiting each other's bodies and living each other's lives the two women must survive in a strange new world.

How will they get back to their own realities… and do they want to? Nothing is ever as it seems as Belisha and Tabitha's lives begin to change forever.

**Order from www.ruthmastersscifi.com or on Amazon.**

Printed in Great Britain
by Amazon